A Cursed English

ROY CULLEN

A Cursed English

tellwell

Tellwell Talent
www.tellwell.ca

ISBN
978-0-2288-3727-5 (Paperback)
978-0-2288-3728-2 (eBook)

ALSO BY ROY CULLEN

Non-fiction

The Poverty of Corrupt Nations

Beyond Question Period, or What really goes on in Ottawa

Table of Contents

Table of Contents, continued

Chapter 1

Le pique-nique, June 1998

That the hamlet of Simiane la Rotonde – perched high on a hill surrounded by glorious fields of lavender – was one of the most charming, picturesque villages imaginable seemed obvious to Nathan and his wife Erika as they approached the age-old entrance gate. On the lavender trail, north of Aix en Provence, and east of Avignon, in Northern Provence, the town dates back to the twelfth century. Erika and Nathan had always wanted to tour Provence, France, and they were very happy to finally be there.

Erika was a retired university educator, originally from South Africa, now a Canadian citizen. Nathan was scaling back his work as a governance consultant with his business partner in Toronto. Prior to that he had worked in senior roles in both business and government. He was born and raised in Montreal. Together Nathan and Erika made a fine-looking pair – gregarious and energetic.

The weather that day, and during their stay up until now, had been magnificent, with mostly sun and warm conditions. Finding a suitable picnic spot in Simiane la Rotonde, however, was another matter. These ancient European towns perched on hillocks are often paved in stone throughout, and this was the challenge. Seeking someone for directions to an area nearby where they could be seated and take in the view while at the same time enjoy their bottle of French wine, purchased that morning at a local vineyard, and their cheese-laden baguettes, proved equally daunting. The place seemed deserted until voices could be heard emanating from a residence located next to the public walkway. Nathan edged closer to the source of the spirited conversation and determined that a small group of men, situated behind an entrance door blocked only by a series of loose beaded strings, was the target of his enquiry. Poking his head through the beads, he enquired, in his best French, about the whereabouts of a picnic spot nearby.

"Excusez-moi, pouvez-vous m'aider s'il vous plais? Mon épouse et moi, nous cherchons un endroit ou nous pourrions avoir une pique-nique. Est-ce qu'il est un parc prés d'ici ou on peut faire ça?"

The three men greeted Nathan, invited him into the small den, and responded in unison, to Nathan's surprise, in English, that there was no such area in the small town for such activities. In the course of the continuing conversation Nathan learned that these three men had been congregating annually for many years in this same town, as a gregarious ritual, and as a means of staying current with each other. One was an Englishman, another American, and the third, un Français, Serge Dubois, the local host. All three were professors or similar professionals. The discussion was flowing very freely when somewhat spontaneously Serge spoke up.

"Why don't you have your picnic on my balcony? From there you will have a wonderful view of the lavender fields and it would be my pleasure for you to enjoy this spot."

"Very kind of you to offer, but we couldn't impose on you in that way," was Nathan's first response.

"Not a problem at all," replied Serge in perfect English, "the three of us were about to take a walk, so the patio balcony is yours. Please come with me."

After a few more attempts by Nathan and Erika to refuse this generosity, the die was cast and up the stairs to the balcony they went. Serge provided a pitcher of spring water for them and they were told that there was a toilet through the door off the balcony that they were free to use.

A large grey and white cat approached and rubbed against Nathan's leg in welcome.

"Don't mind her, she will try to get some of your lunch, but otherwise she's harmless."

Nathan and Erika produced a litany of thank yous before the three men left them to enjoy their lunch. The air was clean and fresh, the weather sunny and warm, and the ambiance unforgettable. Their lunch finished, and with more to explore, Nathan opened the back door to use the bathroom. Inside was a charming cottage that, somewhat out of character in a twelfth century setting, was loaded with leading-edge technologies – from computers to fax machines to servers, to stereo systems. Nathan and Erika marvelled at this dichotomy and contrast in ages. As an example, the walls were thirteen inches thick – a reminder of the century's old origin of the building.

When Serge and friends returned from their walk, the five of them enjoyed a wide-ranging discussion covering a multitude of topics. Nathan and Erika enquired about Serge's hi-tech quarters and learned that he was a professional translator who worked predominately for the United Nations. The United Nations in Geneva, New York, Vienna, or elsewhere, downloaded files to Serge, he would translate them, and upload the result back to the UN. Needless to say, Serge was multi-lingual and he had the perfect virtual office. He could have been situated anywhere, but he chose, not surprisingly, to live and work in the quiet hamlet of Simiane la Rotonde.

Nathan and Erika learned from Serge that, until recently, Northern Province had been a location designated by the French Government for missile silos. It was for this reason that Northern Province had not been actively promoted as a tourist destination point by the national government, unlike Southern Provence.

Serge expanded, "The fewer tourists in the north, in a way, up until now the better. Foreigners nosing around French missile silos were not encouraged. The upside to this policy was that in lieu of tourists, the numerous missile silo installations were the source of employment for the local citizens. Recently, however, the French Government decided that the missile silo operations in the area are to be shut down, and Northern Provence would be marketed to international tourists."

Would this not negatively impact the peaceful enjoyment of the residents of Simiane la Rotonde and surrounds Serge and his colleagues worried? To add insult to injury, as an alternative, a French helicopter company, HELIVOL, was examining the feasibility of using Northern Provence as a low-flying flight-testing area for new helicopters manufactured in Aix en Provence farther south.

"We have been actively lobbying against the helicopter idea but the loss of missile silo jobs is preoccupying the local population. There are some locals who are in favour of the helicopter plan as a way of replacing the silo jobs, but others who worry about the noise and environmental degradation such a scheme might produce. We see the project as something that will spoil the idyllic setting in Northern Provence that we value so much," Serge added.

"Surely low-level helicopter test flights are not the answer for this beautiful area," Nathan offered.

"We have been picketing local government locations, the helicopter company's headquarters, and writing letters to editors of newspapers protesting HELIVOL's plans. Reluctantly we have become political activists."

"What about developing Northern Provence into an area rich in health spas?" Nathan volunteered.

The group liked this idea. They swapped business cards and Nathan promised to investigate the potential interest of Canadian investors in such a development scheme when he returned home. Hands were shaken and as Nathan and Erika left Simiane la Rotonde, they both marvelled at this chance meeting and the positive chemistry that had developed.

Chapter 2

Kathy's Clown

Nathan and Erika were enjoying a sundowner at a charming sidewalk café in Sault, a town not far away from their bed and breakfast hotel in Northern Provence. It was a great location for people-watching.

"Isn't this a great spot?" Erika mused, as she sipped on her glass of Rosé wine from Provence.

A young, attractive woman walking along the sidewalk suddenly caught Nathan's attention. He could have sworn that it was Kathy – a person from Nathan's past. Of course, the mind can play funny tricks. Kathy would now be Nathan's age. Once he came to grips with this, his mind began to wander.

In high school in Montreal in the late 1950's Nathan was really attracted to Kathy, but she had other ideas. How could Kathy be interested in Allan? Allan was tall and good looking but an aura of conceit followed his every move. He wasn't very bright either. Ironically,

Nathan and his friends had an expression that they believed described Allan best – smart-ass! Nathan often wondered if his dislike for Allan was motivated by the fact that he was keeping Kathy from himself. But, upon reflection, Nathan concluded that this was not the case– the guy was a legitimate jerk!

"We can be buddies," Kathy would say.

Nathan would swallow hard and bite his tongue when this topic came up. To have Kathy as his steady girlfriend was Nathan's goal, but that was not to be. That all changed, however, at university where they ended up together on the same campus (not totally by chance) and started dating. They were considered by their peers to be going steady. Allan was off to another university, or maybe he hadn't even bothered to enroll anywhere, so Kathy was fair game. He had seized the moment.

Strange that it was, in high school in a middle-class area, or at least in his area, students were generally assessed not on their academic performance but rather on the freedom from parental control they exhibited, their socializing abilities and on athletic prowess. Being able to pop down to the local soda fountain/deli in the evening during the week to mix and mingle with school friends was considered a badge of honour. You were labelled as cool.

How did they keep up with their school studies? How would they ever get the marks needed to proceed to university? Did they care? Social cliques formed and alliances were made. Nathan was somewhat of an outsider or outlier. He was never considered a cool guy but the fact that he played some football and ice hockey and excelled at schoolwork meant that he was acceptable to most of his peers. Hockey was his first love, but he struggled to become more than an average player. In high school no one was envious of his football talents, in fact at that stage he was a sub-standard player, but while at university under the watchful eye of a great coach, he blossomed into a respectable player such that in his final year he was selected in the Canadian college draft by a professional football team.

In his final year in elementary school, at age twelve, he and a female classmate were awarded modest scholarships for best all-round pupil in the school. At the time, Nathan was of two minds about the award. He was thrilled and flattered to win the award, but at the same time he wondered if he would be seen as uncool.

Fast forward to today and Nathan thought – what nonsense. Fortunately, Nathan, looking back over his career and life to date, could confidentially say that self-improvement had always trumped being cool. Not to say that he was an angel and didn't get into a lot of trouble from time-to-time!

Coming back to Allan, as Nathan continued to enjoy the café setting with Erika, he recalled a situation playing hockey with him. Coaches often assigned the larger players to defence, so that was where Allan was positioned. Nathan was on defence as well, but he was paired with teammate Cliff. On this day they were playing a Francophone team from l'Académie-Louis-Pasteur in their home rink, and their players were fast, mobile and talented. Allan was getting beaten often by the Francophone forwards as they skated extremely fast and nimbly down the wings. He was getting very frustrated. He was looking bad. As a right winger from Académie-Louis-Pasteur flew down the ice, Allan decided enough was enough and he body-checked the winger with an illegal and dirty check. The home crowd erupted with boos and catcalls. Allan spoke French quite well.

"Pea soups!" he yelled.

"Maudit Anglais," reverberated back.

Allan kept playing the same aggressive way. The word was out that a scout from the Montreal Canadiens professional hockey club was in the stands, evaluating Allan and a few other players.

The crowd was on him all the way. Every time Allan touched the puck, the Académie fans booed and hissed. Allan followed a streaking opponent heading towards the blue line. With a quick move, using an illegal body check, he banged the player into the boards headfirst. A moment later Allan was sprawled on the ice with the winger. One of the Académie fans standing by the rink boards, seeing the illegal check, had punched Allan in the chin and for a moment caused him to lose consciousness. Allan was furious and jumped back onto his feet, intending to punch the guilty fan in the face. He stopped in his tracks when he realized the would-be boxer was an elderly *gentilhomme*. Just as well, as the man was ejected from the rink by the security staff.

Allan had a short fuse and easily lost his temper. To add to Nathan's dislike of Allan, Nathan heard through the grapevine that Allan was bad-mouthing him around town and this naturally irritated him. On one occasion

Allan and Nathan had some strong words for each other outside the school, and they almost came to blows.

Fortunately for Nathan, Allan became irrelevant and he was no longer in the picture once Nathan and Kathy arrived at university.

At University, Nathan and Kathy enjoyed each other's company on campus for their freshmen year. Both being in their mid-teens, the decision was made to move on to other relationships. They remained friends, but parted ways. Nathan was a young sixteen-year-old who respected and loved Kathy but he felt that he needed to 'sow his wild oats' before settling down into a more permanent relationship.

Nathan wondered – was their parting a question of conquered love? Was the chase more important than the goal? The word conquering is probably moot, however, since like Catherine of Aragon and Arthur, Henry VIII's elder brother, in the early sixteenth century, their friendship was never consummated!

Chapter 3

Full Moon at University

Nathan and his fraternity friends in the early 1960's had a different idea of what a moon was – and it wasn't the Oxford Dictionary's description of a *natural satellite of a planet.*

It all began on a Sunday morning following a big fraternity party the night before. Fraternities were banned on campus and in the university town, so they were located off-campus in a small village. The fraternity brothers were stuck in the middle of nowhere. There being no food in the refrigerator or cupboards caused their creative juices to flow.

"Let's grab the jeep in the garage and head into town to the corner grocery store and buy some grub," suggested Pierre.

"Great idea," was the unanimous chorus. So off they went in the open-air Jeep.

Driving through the middle of town, the brilliant idea was hatched to pull down their trousers and do a 'moon' – show off their backsides to the locals. Such was the intelligence of young university scholars!

Down went their pants, to the amazement and chagrin of those townsfolk walking the streets and enjoying their Sunday morning. The laughs inside the jeep were loud and raucous. Provisions were acquired at the grocery store and enjoyed later back at the frat house.

The event might have been forgotten, except for a summoning of the Jeep mooners to the university Principal's office a few days later.

The Principal was a respected and affable person, and a big fan of the university football team. The so-called mooners all played on the team so the general feeling was that the sanctions imposed by the Principal would be measured and tolerable. One of the delinquents, Ed, told Nathan that at the upcoming meeting with the Principal, he was worried that he would start to smile or laugh once the Principal started to admonish the group. This struck Nathan as unbelievable, given that the worst-case scenario could be rustication or expulsion.

"You have to be kidding," Nathan turned to Ed.

"Not really," Ed responded.

"Well if that is your attitude, I will do something in the meeting to embarrass you if you act in this way, and try to cover up for you somehow," Nathan asserted.

Nathan could not understand what would motivate Ed to act in this way. It was very puzzling.

Well, the day of the meeting with the Principal finally came around.

Nathan, Ed, Mort, and Pierre crossed the quadrangle and made their way to the Principal's office. Nathan repeated his threat to Ed once more, to deaf ears it seemed. Mort and Pierre shared Nathan's apprehensiveness and concern.

There they were, the four of them, standing in front of the Principal's desk in his tastefully – with a hint of masculinity – decorated office.

He began to read the riot act. Ed and Nathan were standing next to each other when Nathan, through the corner of his eye, noticed that a smile was appearing on Ed's face. With all of the strength that Nathan could muster, he reached behind Ed and pinched him in the rear end as hard as he could. The change in Ed came instantly. Ed flinched and dropped his smiling expression. A calamity had been averted.

The Principal's sanction was measured and very reasonable in the circumstances.

"You will each, the next time you at home visiting with your parents, sit down with them and tell them what you did in a small town near the university, to the great horror and chagrin of the Principal and his staff. This is all that I ask and I will take your word for it that you will do this."

They all breathed a sigh of relief and undertook to do what he had asked. As they were hustled away from the office, Ed was first to say, "Well, that was nothing," he commented. "We don't have to do a thing."

For Nathan it was much more complicated than that. He had given his word to the Principal and he recognized that the Principal had been very fair and generously lenient.

Back in Montreal one weekend to visit his parents, Nathan wrestled with how and when he would break the news about his misbehaviour to his mother and father. Just thinking about it made him break out in a sweat. He was an eighteen-year-old, so coping with this was particularly difficult. On a few occasions he brought himself to the brink of telling them, but the sheer humiliation of it caused him to back off. Finally, he reached the conclusion that he could not honour the commitment he had made to the Principal.

Back at university one week later, Nathan arranged a meeting with the Principal. Once in his office, Nathan remarked, “Sir, I just cannot tell my parents about the mooning incident. Would you please levy another penalty? I am very sorry.”

To which the Principal replied, “Nathan don’t worry about it. We’re all square.”

Later on in life, Nathan began to appreciate the wisdom and maturity of the head of the university. The Principal knew that he had obtained his ‘pound of flesh’. It undoubtedly occurred to the Principal that Nathan had been honest and sincere about honouring the commitment he had made at the meeting when the sanctions were handed out.

Chapter 4

HELIVOL is not amused

Serge and his colleagues in Simiane la Rotonde, decided on an aggressive plan to protest HELIVOL's proposal for test helicopter flights over Northern Provence. They came up with a variety of strategies, including compelling leaflets which they delivered from door-to-door. They covered the rural areas as well as the larger towns like Sault. Social media, while still in relative infancy, was used extensively to get the message out. A web site – HELIVOL NON – was launched and locals were invited to sign a petition that would be presented to the French government, and the National Assembly and Senate. Interest in this campaign was very evident as hundreds signed the petition. Serge had taken the necessary steps to ensure that the petition was in the format required by the *Parlement français* so that the petition, when ready, would not be rejected on technical grounds.

On the weekends, Serge, and the expanding group of protest organizers, picketed outside the HELIVOL factory and head office site in Aix-en-Provence. Opposition to the test flights was growing. Alain Pelletier, the Canadian President of HELIVOL in Aix, and his management team, were countering the protesters with information about how the environmental footprint of the test flights would be minimal, and how jobs would be created for workers in the area should the initiative go ahead. These ideas were not getting a lot of traction with the public-at-large. Firstly, most were of the view that the noise pollution from the low-flying helicopters would be considerable, not to mention any fuel residues or other particles that might drop from the sky. On the jobs front, it was hard for many locals to believe that employment growth arising from the test flights would be significant, if any at all.

One day Mr Pelletier, the HELIVOL President, invited the protesters into his office for a chat. He was accompanied by his VP Public Relations and his objective was obvious – to convince the nay-sayers that the HELIVOL project was a beneficial one. He began the meeting by describing the corporate objectives and the plan for the test flights. He struck most of the protesters as arrogant and obnoxious. He came across as someone condescending to speak with the masses to explain how the world worked. They were not impressed. In fact as the meeting progressed and the group's anger increased, their resolve to stop this project grew. They were provided with the opportunity to present their side of the case, led by Serge Dubois, but they were convinced HELIVOL was not listening. In fact, at one point, Mr Pelletier slammed his fist on the table in an extremely aggressive manner to make a point, further antagonizing the protesters. All in all, this was not a very productive meeting and a precursor of things to come. At one point the President also became physical with one of the protesters. Fortunately, others intervened in a timely manner and a particularly ugly affair was averted.

Mr Pelletier came across as tunnel-visioned and obsessed with his plan to test fly the helicopters over the roofs of the residents of Northern Provence. Compromise was not in the cards. The locals would just have to get used to the idea, in his worldview. The President of the company viewed Serge as the ringleader and chief troublemaker.

Nathan kept in touch with Serge by mail and electronically and followed the developments in Northern Provence closely. He also followed up on his undertaking to research whether there would be any interest by the tourist/spa industry in Canada to invest in hotel and spa infrastructure in Northern Provence. He contacted the Tourism Association of Canada but their focus was largely in attracting tourists to Canada. The management at Fairmont Hotels and Resorts, whose head office was in Toronto, expressed some interest. They had in place the signature Willow Stream Spa concept in many of Fairmont's locations around the world. In Nathan's mind, upscale was the way to go in Northern Province. At first blush, Fairmont struck Nathan as an organization with 'deep pockets'.

The Tigh-Na-Mara Seaside Spa Resort and Conference Centre, located in Parksville, British Columbia featured the world class *Grotto Spa*. Nathan thought they could be a candidate. In the end it was Fairmont that decided to travel to Northern Provence to have a look. Serge arranged a tour of the area for Fairmont's Vice-President of Business Development, Cameron Sutton. Accompanied by Nathan, he organized meetings for the two of them with the local Chambre de Commerce, and with officials in Marseille, the capital of the administrative region of Provence-Alpes-Cote d'Azur. Serge also ensured that Mr Sutton was exposed to his HELIVOL protest group at an informal get-together at the community centre in Simiane la Rotonde. Not surprisingly, Mr Sutton was exposed to some of Provence's finest Rosé wines when they gathered together.

Serge became aware that the President of HELIVOL, Alain Pelletier, knew about the Fairmont VP's presence in Provence, and details of the meetings and arrangements that had been made for him. He had his spies and followed these developments closely.

At the end of his visit, Mr Sutton de-briefed with Serge's group and spoke quite positively of the business opportunities for a luxury spa in Northern Provence. He indicated that it had become obvious that HELIVOL had been lobbying local elected officials and the Chambre de Commerce against any Fairmont investment in the area. Notwithstanding HELIVOL's huge presence in the Aix en Provence area and their obvious political connections, he believed that these dynamics were clearly surmountable.

"Afterall," he commented, "building luxury spas in Northern Provence will bring quality, high-paying jobs; it will bring tourists into the area with money to spend;

and the environmental footprint associated with the spa business will be minimal."

He remained cautiously optimistic. What remained for him to do was to conduct focused market research, and then, assuming positive results, develop a feasibility study and business case for such a project. The next step, if warranted, would be to present an investment proposal to the full executive team at Fairmont, and ultimately to the executive team at Fairmont's holding company – ACCOR Hotels.

As Mr Sutton departed, he and Serge committed to stay in touch. Serge offered to be at his disposal if any local information and/or contacts were required.

When Nathan was organizing this trip to France, it occurred to him that his good friend, Pierre – one of the four who had been disciplined at university many years ago for the infamous mooning incident – had bought a property and built a second home in the outskirts of Avignon, Provence. Pierre and his wife Suzanne were spending four months each year in their new home in Provence. Pierre was born and raised in Quebec City in the Province of Quebec, and Suzanne grew up in France, so they were both fluently bi-lingual. They also loved France, and especially Provence, so this move had not surprised Nathan.

When in France, Nathan took the opportunity to meet with Pierre and Suzanne over dinner in their home in Avignon. It was great to see them and to catch-up on all of their news. Nathan described the initiative he was working on in Northern Provence and why he thought luxury spas would be a great addition to the area. He outlined the connections with Serge and HELIVOL and other background information about the project. Pierre and Suzanne were immediately enthusiastic about the idea, especially in light of the other alternative – low level helicopter test flights flying over their home! They offered to help Nathan with his advocacy efforts. Nathan saw this as a blessing; having a local trusted contact on the ground in Provence, in addition to Serge who was involved and interested in this initiative.

Nathan introduced Pierre and Suzanne to Serge by way of a Skype call so that they could be situated on the same page and fully briefed on the status of this undertaking. Fortunately, the group chemistry was very positive and the parties agreed to stay in touch and work together. Nathan was quite relieved and encouraged to have these local connections, given the fact that he lived in Toronto and could not be flying back and forth to France on a regular basis.

Nathan had to decide how much time, energy, and money he would dedicate to this project. If the Tigh-Na-Mara resort, a smaller business which was privately owned, had been interested there would have been an opportunity perhaps for Nathan to buy into an equity position in the new investment in Provence. With Fairmont involved this possibility probably did not exist. They would go on their own. Nathan, however, still felt committed to moving this initiative forward. He was aligned with the goals of Serge and the group; so, for the time being he would continue his involvement and see how it developed.

Chapter 5

Have a Goat

In the mid 1970's, Nathan, and his newly married first wife, Julia, decided to travel and see some of the world while he still earned a living. He found himself working as a Chartered Accountant in Johannesburg, South Africa.

They loved their garden and the one-acre paddock that housed their two horses. Their young gardener, Solomon Molefe Motsume, was a tireless and competent worker who kept the garden maintained, and looked after the dogs and horses on Nathan and Julia's small property holding. Nathan had fired two other gardeners after finding them asleep on the property when they were supposed to be working. Solomon presented himself at Nathan's door shortly thereafter offering his services. Solomon was a devoutly Christian man from Botswana, so Nathan decided to hire him, and this confidence proved to be well placed.

One little hiccup, however, was that Solomon was in South Africa on a temporary work permit that needed to be renewed three months after he started to work with Nathan. Solomon indicated that this would not be a problem but that at some point he would have to return to Botswana for a few days to renew his visa. This would not be an issue according to Solomon, considering that his brother worked at the South Africa/Botswana border crossing close to Solomon's village.

The day finally arrived when Solomon approached Nathan, "Baas, I need to return to Botswana so that my visa can be renewed. With your permission I will need two days off to travel to Botswana, renew the visa, and return to Johannesburg."

Nathan pondered this for a moment. There were numerous individuals in the area who would gladly be hired to work in Nathan's garden and look after the horses. The nuisance value of Solomon's visa problem caused Nathan to wonder whether he should bother himself with this, or should he simply put the word out that he was looking for a gardener? On the other hand, Solomon was working out well.

"Solomon, OK, go ahead. If you have any problems in Botswana getting a visa, or any other issues, call me on the telephone and we will see if I can help."

Sure enough a few days later the call came through.

"Baas, I am here at the Botswana/South Africa border post where my brother works and everything is going well except that I am told you are needed here to sign an employment contract with me saying that if I get sick, you will look after me. Once that is in place, I will get my visa."

Nathan paused for a moment and quickly decided that he would go and help Solomon, and himself at the same time.

"Where is this border post?" Nathan asked.

Solomon provided the directions to the small out-of-the way border crossing location, not far from a Botswana town named Lobatse, and they decided on the timing given that it was about a four-hour drive to this border crossing.

"I will be standing on the Botswana side of the border gate when you arrive," Solomon stated confidently.

Julia packed a lunch for Nathan and off he drove early the next morning.

Four hours later Nathan safely arrived at the border crossing and was very relieved to see Solomon with a huge smile on his face on the other side of the big gate.

The first stop on the other side of the gate was the Botswana border office dealing with customs and immigration. There, Nathan met Solomon's brother, Poloko, who was standing behind the counter in his uniform. It was at this moment that Nathan was told that the contract was prepared and all was in order; however, it would need to be signed by an elder from Solomon's village – some 20 miles away!

Off they went. Too much was invested now, thought Nathan. The dirt road was dusty and windy, but they finally pulled into an administrative-type building where a chief or otherwise official-looking tribal person happily co-signed Solomon's contract with Nathan.

By this time hunger was gnawing at them so they headed back to the border post. Driving in the car, Solomon turned to Nathan and said, "Baas, I thank God that you took the time to come to Botswana to sign my contract. To show my thanks I would like to present you with a goat."

"My goodness Solomon, that is very kind but not necessary at all."

Nathan was very conscious of the need to be sensitive and to show appreciation for this gift. He needed a goat like he needed a hole in his head.

"Where is this goat?" Nathan enquired.

Without hesitation, Solomon informed Nathan, "It is at my Mother's home."

"And where might that be?"

"It is about twenty-five miles from here," informed Solomon. But, as luck would have it, her home was in the opposite direction from where they were headed.

Feeling some relief, Nathan turned to Solomon and told a little white lie, "It would be great to have this goat but I must get back to Johannesburg today and there will not be enough time to do this."

Solomon appeared to take this news philosophically and seemed to understand the logistics. They continued on their way to the border and parked in front of Poloko's home, a small and modest house in walking distance to his office, the border post, and surrounded by a wire fence. Solomon invited Nathan into Poloko's home for some lunch. Nathan thanked Solomon and agreed to join them inside but indicated that he would eat the sandwiches that his wife had packed for him. Opening the gate, Nathan was surrounded by several clucking chickens that moved around Poloko's property at great speed.

After seating himself in the living room, Nathan heard the unmistakable sound of a hen being chased, its throat slit, and plucked. This naked bird was presented to Nathan jointly by Solomon and Poloko as a gift of appreciation. Nathan thanked them profusely (he was getting the knack of this) and stuffed the bird into the trunk of his car. He pondered briefly whether it was legal to take meat across the border to South Africa, but que sera, sera.

Onwards to the border post. Poloko headed out the back door of his house and magically was behind the counter at Botswana's customs and immigration outpost in a flash when Solomon and Nathan arrived. The contract was presented and stamped with official stamps by Solomon's brother it seemed like a hundred times – making everything official and resoundingly approved.

But not so fast. The South African border officer at the next stop a few meters further on had a different take on the matter. Nathan explained the story about the contract, the reliable and hardworking qualities demonstrated by Solomon, and the desire to contract with him formally for a period initially of two years. Nathan also made the point that he had driven from Johannesburg earlier that day to Botswana to complete this deal.

The South African border official looked at the signed and sealed contract briefly and blurted out, "This contract must be signed in Pretoria."

Pretoria is the administrative capital of South Africa, but this made no sense at all. Nathan appealed to the official's superior, but to no avail.

As Nathan headed into the sunset on his own, Solomon undertook to return to Johannesburg, with the help of his brother, on another temporary work permit.

Nathan was disappointed and angry, but what could he do.

One evening back in Johannesburg he and Julia were invited around to dinner at their friends' home. The husband, Gerard, was a stereotypical Afrikaner, albeit more progressive than many of that clan. Nathan told him of his recent experience with Solomon and his trip to Botswana.

"Easily solved," stated Gerard. "I have a good friend who works in Bantu Administration in Randburg. You should use my name and make an appointment to go and see him. Take a bottle of scotch with you to give to him and *Bob's your uncle,*" finished Gerard.

Nathan had never bribed anyone and he felt very uncomfortable doing this. Discomfort set aside for the moment, off he went at the appointed hour to meet with Mr Hanse van der Merwe. He met a dead end here also. He was told by Mr van der Merwe that retirement was only two months away and he was not willing to take any more chances at the looming end of his civil service career. He had another suggestion, however. Captain Arnold Benadie at the South African Police station at John Vorster Square could help Nathan.

A few days later Nathan set up the appointment with Captain Benadie but he was very anxious and nervous.

John Vorster Square had a very scary reputation. A prisoner having been thrown out of twelfth floor windows, allegedly by a police officer, was one of stories reported in the news.

This may be my last resort, rationalized Nathan; besides the police station was just a few blocks away from his office. Why not give it a try?

During a lunch break he readily passed security given his pre-arranged meeting and found himself in an elevator heading to the seventh floor at John Vorster Square. He was escorted into the Captain's office.

Nathan made his pitch.

Captain van der Merwe's face turned beet red.

"Who told you to come and see me about this? Who gave you my name?" he shouted at Nathan.

At this point Nathan decided that, unless he was taken to the rack or whipped one hundred times, he would not betray his sources.

Nathan evaded the question which the Captain repeated over and over again. Not making any progress, the Captain pointed to his office door and exclaimed, "This meeting is over!"

Nathan made a hasty retreat, considering himself lucky to be able to head back to his office for the afternoon.

Solomon walked slowly down the driveway to Nathan's home a few days later, having returned from Botswana and happily showing off his temporary work visa which was newly stamped in his identity document.

They both realized that this was a temporary fix. Two months later Solomon approached Nathan in the garden and informed him that he had it on good information that a permanent work visa could be obtained in the nearby township of Alexandria with the payment of a modest fee of fifty rand. What to lose, Nathan thought. I would spend fifty rand on a beer. He gave Solomon the cash and crossed his fingers. His hopes were realized when Solomon appeared a few days later with the needed stamp in his identity document. What a relief!

They had come around full circle, but the mission had been accomplished. Solomon worked with Nathan and Julia for many years thereafter. For Nathan this was an important life experience. It taught him the value of staying committed to an outcome and having the patience to see projects through to their successful conclusion. Tactics may need to be altered to reach a desired end point. In addition, another lesson learned was that often-serendipitous events can intervene and help one achieve a goal, albeit in a different way.

Chapter 6

The letter

Nathan had put the spa project on the backburner as he waited for Fairmont to complete their analysis. He was a partner in a boutique management consulting company, so that kept him busy. He and Erika enjoyed an active social life rounding out their well-balanced lives.

All of that changed, however, one day when Nathan went to check the mail at home and discovered a letter addressed to him from an unexpected source. The letter was from Serge's brother Jacques Dubois – someone Nathan had never met or knew anything about. The letter was postmarked from Paris and written in longhand in French. Fortunately, Nathan's facility with the French language allowed him to read and understand what Jacque's message was.

le 8 Juin, 1999
Paris, France +33 9 81 89 39 93
cher Nathan;

I trust this finds you well.
I am writing this letter to you because I know that you had a chance encounter with my brother Serge in Simiane la Rotonde a year ago, and that, since then, you have been in communication with him. I bring you some bad news. Serge was involved in a motor car accident outside the town of Sault in Provence and he was not able to recover from his serious injuries. He died on May 20. He spoke so highly of you and I know that he would have wanted me to communicate with you to tell you the news. I live in Paris, but I was interested in Serge's protest movement because it is such a worthwhile cause. He and I spoke on the telephone on many occasions and he kept me up to date on his and your efforts. In keeping with Serge's wishes, there was no funeral.
Hopefully our paths will cross somehow, someday. . . .

Sincèrement,
Jacques Dubois

Nathan put down the letter and was saddened, and shocked into disbelief. It was so difficult to come to grips with the reality that someone, who until very recently, was fit and healthy, was no longer alive.

Nathan jotted down a short sympathy note in longhand to Jacques, obviously Jacques' communication method of choice, and told him that he would make some enquiries with others in the protest group, and he would call a friend of his who lived in Avignon to try and make some sense of this and its impact on the helicopter protest initiative. Nathan undertook to keep Jacques informed of any developments, and he asked Jacques to do the same.

Nathan picked up the telephone and dialed Pierre in Avignon. Suzanne answered and they had a chat about several things. Solving the world's problems over the telephone preoccupied them for some time between other pleasantries.

Suzanne brought up the topic that was covered in a magazine article that she had just read about how corruption was rampant in Russia. The article concluded by stating that President Putin was possibly the richest man, or one of the richest, in the world.

"Suzanne, I couldn't agree more; and what is even more troubling is that the situation in that country is getting worse, not better."

Nathan was told that Pierre was out and about somewhere, but Suzanne promised that she would tell him about the call and that Pierre would call back as soon as possible. She anticipated that he would be back home shortly.

A few minutes later the phone rang.

"Hi Nathan. I'm sorry I missed your earlier call but had to run a few errands – you know how it is," said Pierre.

"Not a problem. How are things in Avignon?"

"All is well here. We are enjoying some great weather and taking the opportunity to hike in the area. Yesterday we walked the Paul Cézanne Trail in Aix en Provence which was amazing. How is everything with you?"

"All is well, but I just learned that Serge died on May 20th following a motor car accident outside the town of Sault. I am stunned and saddened by this."

"Come to think about it, there was a brief article about the accident that I read some days ago in *La Provence,* the daily Marseille newspaper. I hadn't connected the dots. What a tragedy."

"It would be interesting to know whether the Police Nationale, or the Sault Police Municipale, is investigating the accident. I am curious about the incident and how it happened. Serge's brother Jacques provided no details," Nathan asserted.

"Yes, I will place a telephone call to Sault and get that information and I will get back to you," Pierre responded.

"Merci beaucoup mon ami. I look forward to your call."

Chapter 7

"Knowing yourself is the beginning of all wisdom." – Aristotle

Nathan pondered what he had just learned about Serge and thought to himself how fortunate he had been in his life. Nathan was alive and well, healthy, enjoying life, and at the apex of his career and, by way of contrast, Serge was dead at the age of forty.

After finishing an undergraduate degree, Nathan had decided in 1971 to complete his studies in accounting by articling with a Chartered Accountancy firm in Hamilton, Bermuda. This had been quite an adventure for him, and something he yearned for and looked forward to doing. He had joined a medium-sized practice that did work with local clients as well as agency work for three of the big international accounting firms. Clients included local retail businesses, resorts, and golf clubs, together with a combination of offshore businesses including captive insurance companies, mutual funds, and what are often described as *paper tigers*.

Nathan recalled an interesting set of events associated with a wholly owned subsidiary of a Calgary-based oil and gas company. The company, Brontosaurus Oil Indonesia, an audit client, whose holding company, Triceratops, was listed on the Calgary and New York stock exchanges, was incorporated to own and operate Triceratop's business interests in Indonesia. Brontosaurus Oil Indonesia was drilling for oil in that country and had entered into an agreement with the Indonesian state-owned company, PERTAMINA. The income from any payable oil or gas discovered would be shared 50/50 between the two entities. As it happened, drilling in one area was very successful and the oil reserves were significant enough to justify drilling derricks, and installing a pipeline to a port where it would be loaded and shipped to locations around the world. Indonesian oil is generally considered to be very high-quality oil because of its low sulfur content. The race was on to build the pipeline and start pumping.

Brontosaurus Oil Indonesia was incorporated in Bermuda and had its head office in the nation's capital, Hamilton. Bermuda is a tax haven and free of corporate income tax. As a result of this, income accruing to Brontosaurus Oil Indonesia would be tax-free and could be used to finance other Triceratops projects around the world using pre-tax dollars. Nathan understood that Bermuda was a tax haven but he was also conscious of the fact that the Government of Bermuda strongly discouraged dirty money being laundered in their island country. Funds and operations were located there to avoid taxes, which is legal because it involves working within the existing laws and rules for maximum advantage, as opposed to tax evasion, which is illegal. Certainly, there were some companies, individuals and trusts set up in Bermuda to evade taxes, but in his time on the island Nathan saw no evidence of dirty money deposited or invested there that was derived from drugs, people smuggling, human trafficking, terrorist financing or other heinous crimes.

Brontosaurus Oil Indonesia's head office was located in a small cubby-hole-like office in Hamilton, that housed one desk and one employee. Millions of dollars of oil revenue from the Indonesian operations started flowing through the company once the oil was pumping and getting shipped to various customers abroad. The one employee of Brontosaurus Oil Indonesia received periodic journal entries from the Calgary head office of Triceratops, together with minutes from management meetings and meetings of the Board of Directors. These were all pasted into the appropriate register.

There is a provision in Canada's *Income Tax Act* that provides that if the direction and control of a company is deemed to be derived from Canada, then the profits of that company are taxable in Canada. It didn't take a genius to conclude that the direction and control of Brontosaurus Oil Indonesia came from the holding company's head office in Calgary. One day, representatives from the Canada Revenue Authority (CRA) descended unannounced at the offices of the holding company in Calgary and proceeded to conduct an audit. Three days later they served a tax assessment of some nine million dollars on the company, and, at the same time, froze several of the company's bank accounts. The claim? No surprise – that the direction and control of Brontosaurus Oil Indonesia came from Canada, and that therefore their profits were taxable in Canada.

Triceratops scrambled to find the best firm of tax lawyers in Canada and they soon came upon Spikeman and Ellis. The law firm carefully reviewed the income tax assessment and analyzed how Brontosaurus Oil Indonesia operated.

"You can't win the direction and control argument because clearly the company was managed from Calgary," the lead lawyer, Ben Spikeman advised.

"If, however, we assume for the moment that the profits are taxable in Canada then it follows that the company would be eligible to claim the investment tax credits currently available, and other favourable tax features like accelerated capital cost allowances and others," he said.

"We have re-computed the income tax return as assessed by the CRA and by taking advantage of these legitimate tax credits and allowances, the company ends up with a loss carry forward for the period in question!" remarked Ben.

Not surprisingly, when this was brought to the attention of the Canada Revenue Agency, they dropped the tax assessment and unfroze the bank accounts.

Nathan had followed this process carefully, and he was fascinated with the end result. One aspect was the fact that in going through the books of Brontosaurus

Oil Indonesia Nathan came across an amount of over one million US dollars that was paid into a Swiss bank account. Upon further enquiry he learned that this was paid to an Indonesian Army General – a bribe to cover the protection of the pipeline. Nathan was aghast but was told that this is how business is done in Indonesia. Later on in Nathan's career, this act of bribery was a key motivating factor that prompted him to seriously engage in the global fight against corruption.

Another offshore client of Nathan's was a so-called *paper tiger* – Triangle Chemicals – the wholly-owned subsidiary of an enormous multi-national chemical company, Potash plc, based in the United Kingdom. The way it worked was as follows. All sales from Potash plc's many plants around the world were invoiced to Triangle Chemicals but shipped directly to the customer. As Nathan learned, the trick is in what is called transfer pricing. In the office, Nathan turned to a colleague, Ned, who specialized in taxation.

"How does transfer pricing work?" Nathan enquired.

"In cases like this the objective is to keep as much of the profit margins in Bermuda, where they won't be taxed," replied Ned.

"Doesn't the British Government care when they miss out on profits that could be taxed in the UK?"

"Oh yes, they do care. Companies in the UK must sell, or buy, products or services to affiliated companies at prices that approximate fair market value. Her Majesty's Revenue & Customs Department monitors this closely."

Ned continued, "The reality is that determining fair market value involves estimates and judgement calls.

Also, there is typically a range of what price would constitute fair market value. So, for example, the fair market value of one metric ton of sulphuric acid could be in the range of £36 - £40. What Potash plc would do is sell the acid to Triangle Chemicals for £36 per metric ton. Triangle Chemicals would then immediately turn around and sell the sulphuric acid to the group's ultimate customer for £40. In that way a good chunk of the profit margin stays tax free in Bermuda. Her Majesty's Revenue & Customs Department's hands would effectively be tied, because the price is in the range of fair market value."

"I see now why these companies in Bermuda are called paper tigers," commented Nathan.

It seemed to Nathan that this model, generally considered to qualify as tax avoidance, bordered on fitting the definition of tax evasion. But what did he know? He was just a rookie accountant.

It was not all work and no play for Nathan, however, in Bermuda.

Prior to leaving for Bermuda Nathan had started to play rugby in Montreal and he was given some rugby names and contacts to look up in Bermuda. Before you knew it, he was suited up and on the roster of a local rugby side, the Rogues, in Bermuda. He immediately connected with three of his teammates, Nick, Vincent and Dave, *the boys,* as they were called. They quickly became inseparable. Nick, Vincent, and Dave shared a flat together notwithstanding their varied backgrounds, Nick was British, Vincent hailed from Gibraltar, and Dave was Australian. Nathan lived on his own.

Soon after Nathan's arrival in Bermuda *the boys* insisted on a photo shoot out by the airport. Nathan stood on a wooden soap box behind Nick's sports car, which, from the other side, gave the impression that Nathan was six feet, eight inches tall. Height is very important for a second-row lock forward, especially for the lineouts. Photos were taken from different angles.

"Now", said Nick, "we will circulate these photos around to the three other rugby clubs and tell them that the Rogues have acquired a six foot, eight inch Canadian lock forward, or second row scrum player, and he will be on the pitch for the next game coming up in one week. This will freak them out!"

This type of gesture was very typical of how they operated. Many laughs were shared during Nathan's two year stay on the island. Nathan was exposed to a new vocabulary. He would be asked around to *the boys* flat for an *HD*. He soon learned that *the boys* were Nick, Vincent & Dave; and *HD* was a hot dinner. Nathan was asked to assemble a 'party-goers kit'. He learned later that this was a tongue-in-cheek description of an assemblage of three items – a rope, a whistle, and a pair of runners – all designed to assist with speedy exits scaling fence walls from parties that the boys and Nathan would crash! Many an entertaining evening were spent at the Hoppin' John pub on Front Street, the Rogues watering hole.

Dave, the Aussie, often stood up at parties and recited this *down-under* poem called *The Spider by the*

Gwydir, to howls of laughter, using his thickest home-grown Australian accent.

By the sluggish river Gwydir lived a hungry red-
backed spider,
Who was just about as mean as could be;
An' the place that he was camped in was an empty
Jones's jam tin
In a paddock near the showgrounds, at Moree.
Near him lay a shearer snoozin', who'd been on beer
an' boozin'
All that night and all the previous day;
An' the rookin' of the rookers an' the noise of
showground spruikers
Failed to wake him from the daze in which he lay.

Then a crafty-lookin' spieler with a dainty little Sheila
Came along, collectin' wood to make a fire.
Said the spieler, "He's a boozer, an' he's goin' to be a loser;
If he isn't you can christen me a liar."
"Hustle round and keep nit, honey, while I fan the
mug for money
And we'll have some dainty luxuries for tea."
But she answered, "Don't be silly; you go back and
boil the billy,
You can safely leave the mug to little me."

So she circled ever nearer till she reached the dopey
shearer
With his pockets bulgin', fast asleep and snug;
But she didn't see the spider that was ringin' close
beside her

For her mind was on the money an' the mug.
The spider sighted dinner. He'd been daily growin'
thinner;
He'd been fastin' an' was hollow as an urn.
As she eyed the bulgin' pocket, he just darted like a rocket
An' bit the spieler's Sheila on the stern.

Then the Sheila started squealin' an' her clothes she
was unpeelin',
To hear her yells would make you feel forlorn.
One hand the bite was pressin' while the other was
undressin'
An' she reached the camp the same as she was born.
Then the shearer, pale an' haggard, woke, an' back to
town he staggered
Where he caught the train an' gave the booze a rest;
An' he'll never know the spider that was camped
beside the Gwydir
Had saved him sixty smackers of the best.

Part of the humour was how Dave delivered the poem in his very exaggerated accent. Nathan memorized the poem as he was fascinated with it, and from time-to-time he would recite it. He remembered one occasion in particular, when he and Erika were on a European river cruise, and they met up with some Australians. Nathan, over drinks after dinner on the ship, rendered the poem aloud, in his best Aussie voice imitation. They were amazed that a Canadian knew this poem, and they all shrieked with laughter.

Chapter 8

Allô police

Nathan ran from his garage to answer the phone.

"Hello Nathan, this is Pierre."

"Hi Pierre, good to hear your voice."

"My apology for taking so long in getting back to you, but it has been somewhat of a struggle getting answers from the authorities in Sault."

Pierre continued, "I finally got through to someone who told me that the car crash that Serge was involved in is being handled by the Sault Police Municipale, and not the Police Nationale. I initially thought this was somewhat strange, but upon further review I established that motor vehicle accidents are typically done this way, even those with fatalities."

"Were you able to speak with someone in the Sault Police Municipale about the accident?" enquired Nathan.

"Yes, I spoke with a Constable Henri Paquette. He seemed to be the police officer assigned to this file. He gave me a hard time initially about providing details of the accident because I wasn't a relative but my friend's friend, or a friend twice removed. Once you called Jacques – Serge's brother in Paris – and Jacques spoke to Constable Paquette and gave his approval for him to provide me with the information, he was more forthcoming and cooperative. Thanks for doing that. It also helped considerably that Jacques had previously traveled to Simiane la Rotunde and Sault upon learning of his brother's death to settle some of Serge's affairs and in that process he had met briefly with Constable Paquette."

"Great, glad that worked. Did he describe the accident and how it happened?"

"Yes, he provided a general description. He said the accident happened at 7 pm on May 19. It appeared that Serge was driving from Sault to Simiane la Rotunde following a visit to a local grocery store to pick up some food. There was a grocery bag in the damaged car. The drive from Sault to Simiane la Rotunde is about 22 kilometers driving southeast all the way on Highway D – 30."

"What were the driving conditions like? Did he say?"

"Apparently the weather was clear and the temperature was about eighteen degrees Celsius. Sunset that day was at 8 pm so Serge was driving in the light. There had been no recent precipitation so the roads were clear. It sounds like the driving conditions were excellent. The Constable said that speed, alcohol or drugs were not factors in the accident, but you know how fast they drive in la France!"

"How did the accident happen?" Nathan enquired.

"There was a curve in the road and it sounds like Serge missed the turn and drove onto the gravel shoulder. He then lost control and veered into the ditch, finally crashing into a large tree. There was no air bag in his earlier model car. He suffered severe blows to the head, to which he finally succumbed the next day. A passing motorist came across the accident five to ten minutes after the incident and immediately called the police. He was rushed to the closest hospital in Apt, a town about one half hour from the scene of the accident. Doctors at the hospital put him into an induced coma to deal with the swelling in the brain. But in the end it was not enough."

"It would be useful to get a copy of the police report of the accident," Nathan suggested.

"I agree. I will request this from Constable Paquet and get back to you. Do you have a fax machine he could send it to?"

"Yes, I do."

Nathan gave Pierre the number.

"By the way, when I spoke with Jacques I discovered that he is quite conversant in English. He had written the letter to me in French so I had wondered."

"Bon. À la prochaine," they concluded.

Chapter 9

Down on the Farm

A few days later Pierre called Nathan.

"I just had a call back from Constable Paquette in Sault in response to my request for a copy of the accident report. He said it shouldn't be a problem but he is just checking with his boss. I just thought I would let you know where it is at," said Pierre.

"Merci. Let me know when you hear back. Otherwise, what else is new?"

"Well, the lavender is just beginning to flower here in Avignon and it is truly magnificent. The rows upon rows of dusky purple lavender, and their sweet scent cascading over the fields is a delight to the senses. A far cry from my uncle's dairy farm in rural Québec where the *sweet* smell of manure was more prevalent!" commented Pierre.

"Interesting. Where was the farm? Did you visit it often?"

"My father, together with his seven siblings, was born and raised on this farm about a one-hour drive south of Montreal. Interestingly, the farm was located on the exact site of the Battle of Châteauguay which took place during the War of 1812 between British and US forces, when the British twarted an attempt by the Americans to capture Montreal. Shortly after this battle, around 1813 or 1814, my great grandfather emigrated from Scotland and started to farm on this property."

"In any case, let's get back to the twentieth century! Over time, all my father's brothers and sisters left the farm for greener pastures – no pun intended – leaving my uncle Jack and my grandmother holding the fort, so to speak. It was a mixed farm, largely dairy, with about twenty producing dairy cows. During my school years I often joined my uncle on the farm to help him during the haying season," chronicled Pierre.

"That must have been interesting. Did you enjoy your time there?"

"Uncle Jack was somewhat eccentric and he had a horrible temper. Otherwise it was something different and it was fun. There are a few stories!"

"Tell me some stories. You have piqued my curiosity."

"I remember one summer in particular. My uncle and I were out together with the tractor and the mower to cut hay in the fields. When we had finished Uncle Jack uncoupled the mower from the tractor. He turned to me and said, "Pierre, tomorrow I would like you to come back here on the tractor on your own and mow the two adjacent fields over there. Your grandma will pack you a lunch so you can stay out here all day. When you have finished, unhook the mower and leave it in the field.

Come back to the farm on the tractor and be back to the farmyard before it gets dark."

Pierre paused as he remembered.

"I was elated. He had put his faith in me, as a young teenager, to get the work done and act responsibly. I was making a real contribution. The next morning I left the farm early, with my lovingly packed lunch, and headed across the quiet highway that ran in front of the farm and onto the hay fields. The weather was perfect as I hooked up the mower to the tractor and began to cut hay. At midday, perched on the tractor seat, I enjoyed my lunch and then proceeded to the next field."

"At the end of the day having completed mowing the second field, and remembering my uncle's instructions, I pulled out a wrench from the tractor toolbox so that I could uncouple the mower and leave it in the field. The bolt would not budge! I worked at it and tried and tried, but to no avail. Having noticed a hack saw in the toolbox, I began to saw the thick bolt as my last alternative. Although dusk was upon us, it was still very warm and I perspired profusely until finally the bolt was in two pieces and the mower was sitting on its own. I chucked the severed bolt into a ditch to destroy the evidence!"

"Quickly I jumped on the tractor and headed back to the farmyard. It was getting dark as I crossed the sleepy highway. Sure enough, at the top of the road to the farmyard, stood my uncle, not looking very happy."

"I told you to be back here before dark, and look at you," he yelled.

"My uncle proceeded to ream me out for a few minutes. I just listened in the silent knowledge that my mission, apart from a couple of hiccups, had been accomplished."

"Quite the experience for a young fella!" Nathan commented.

"Yes, and another time I ripped a tool shed door off its tracks when I was running the tractor back and forth while my uncle was stacking hay in the hay mow in the barn using a grapple hook controlled with ropes and pulleys. Uncle Jack was not amused, to put it mildly."

"Notwithstanding these incidents, my uncle and I had a solid and positive relationship and I worked on the farm over many summers, sometimes just helping with the milking," concluded Pierre.

"Interestingly, lavender in Provence is also harvested mechanically with machines hooked up to tractors, as I discovered during our stay there. The machines cut the stems in lengths that are designed to promote new growth. There are probably similar stories to tell from that area as well."

"Enjoy Avignon. Oh, while I think of it, and before you go, my classmates and I used to often sing this song in French class at school in Montreal."

Nathan took a deep breath and sang.

"Sur le pont d'Avignon,
L'on y danse, l'on y danse,
Sur le pont d'Avignon
L'on y danse tout en rond"

"You must know this famous song," Nathan asserted, after singing the tune somewhat off key.

"Yes, certainly. Le Pont Saint-Bénézet is the other name for this bridge that was originally built in the 12th century. It is quite an historical landmark that we enjoy visiting from time-to-time," Pierre commented.

"All for now. Let me know when you hear back from Constable Paquette."

"Bien sûr," Pierre ended.

Chapter 10

"Information is not knowledge." – Albert Einstein

Pierre telephoned Nathan a few days later.

"I heard back from Constable Paquette, and the news is not good."

"What did he say?"

"He told me that he checked with his boss, the Chief of Police in Sault, Captain Édouard Mercier, who told him that the accident report, for reasons of privacy, cannot be released," Pierre answered.

"That doesn't make any sense," stated Nathan.

"You are right. Surely it is in the public interest to make this report available to interested parties."

"The only exception I can think of is if the release of this information would pose a threat to national security. Surely that is not the case here. In Canada we have strong Access to Information laws and I believe that France has a very strong regime in this area as well. In fact, if you don't mind, and if you can spare a few moments, I can check on-line what the situation is in France with respect to access to information. Can you bear with me?" Nathan asked.

"Absolutely," said Pierre.

The phone line went silent for a few minutes while Nathan googled the information.

Nathan came back on the line.

"Pierre, here is what it says about access to information in France. Firstly, we are told that, and this is a direct quote – 'In France, the accountability of public servants is a constitutional right, according to the *Declaration of the Rights of Man and of the Citizen.*' The French government brought in enabling legislation which establishes the general rule 'that citizens can demand a copy of any administrative document in paper, digitised or other form'."

Nathan paused for a moment as he checked the computer screen in front of him and then continued.

"There is an administrative body – *La Commission d'Accès aux Documents Administratifs*, which translates as follows, the *Commission for Access to Administrative Documents*. This Commission is an independent administrative authority that oversees the process and interprets the declaration and the law."

"All of this sounds very positive for what we wish to achieve," commented Pierre.

"Yes, I agree," Nathan confirmed. "It sounds almost tailor-made to our requirements. From reading through the material on the web site, it sounds to me like a formal letter must be sent to the administrative body as a first step requesting the documents in question. The administrative body, in this case the Sault Municipal Police, is then required to respond in writing. If, at that point, the police department refuses to share the accident report with us, we can then appeal to the *Commission for Access to Administrative Documents*."

"Sounds good. I wonder if it would be more powerful if that request, in writing, came from Serge's brother, Jacques, in Paris?" pondered Pierre.

"Absolutely. Good point. I will contact Jacques and ask him if he will do that. I can draft up a letter for him," said Nathan.

"Productive discussion. Onwards and upwards. We need to pursue this, for Serge's sake if nothing else. Keep me posted," commented Pierre.

"Will do. Au revoir."

Chapter 11

Race to the top

The weather in Toronto had taken a turn for the worse. Nathan was sprawled on the couch in the family room of his home reading the newspaper and allowing his mind to wander. He reflected on his experience working in South Africa. Initially the motivation had been, as a newly qualified Chartered Accountant, to see Africa from a strong industrial base where one could learn and grow professionally. Accounting firms in South Africa were recruiting aggressively, making the economics favourable as well.

Nathan had some wonderful memories from his time there from 1973 to 1977. The only difficult part of living in South Africa was coping with the apartheid policy that was in place. One learned to work around this and do what one could in a small way to contribute to positive experiences between people of different races and colours. Of course, nowadays the situation in South Africa is completely different with the release of Nelson Mandela in 1990 resulting in the multiracial general election in 1994, his election as President, and the dismantling of apartheid.

In 1973 Nathan and three audit managers had the responsibility to schedule work assignments, provide mentorship to articling students, review audit files and evaluate the performance of a group of sixty employees. Each individual manager had the specific role of providing human resource support to fifteen staff, the typical *rum & rations* model. The public accounting practice, which employed three hundred personel, was large by Johannesburg standards, and a highly successful one. The firm had largely cornered the audit market on the iconic public companies. On the audit side, Nathan's shared group of sixty was replicated four times over.

One of Nathan's clients, Saphire Holdings, was a listed public company with diversified interests that were concentrated in the music industry in southern Africa. The partner who Nathan reported to on this job, Rob Potts, was a highly intelligent and progressive individual. He and Nathan got along well.

One day Rob popped into Nathan's office.

"Our firm has just hired a person of colour to join our ranks as an articling student. Amazingly this step is a first for this country. Jeff Moshaka will be the first black African articling student in this country. He recently graduated with an undergraduate degree in business from the University of the North in the Eastern Transvaal. As you know, this is a university for black Africans. He is an exceptional person and my partners and I have decided that we would like to place him under your wing and join your audit group. What do you think?"

"I am flattered that you would have the confidence in me to ask me to handle this. Of course, I will do it. I will be delighted," replied Nathan.

"Great. We thought you would willingly and eagerly take this on. Given that the Sapphire Holdings audit is coming up very soon. I suggest we start Jeff on this assignment," Rob stated.

"I couldn't agree more. We will need to give the senior management team at Sapphire a heads-up and make sure they are on board. Having a multi-racial audit team on site will be quite different," offered Nathan.

"Absolutely. I will call the President and VP Finance today and let you know what they say. Knowing the personalities there, I believe they will be very supportive."

Later that day, Rob confirmed that there was no difficulty at all. Sapphire Management had enthusiastically agreed with their proposition. It was hard to imagine that this level of clearance was necessary, but the politics in South Africa at that time made this a very delicate issue.

Upon arrival at Sapphire Holdings, Nathan introduced the audit team to the company's VP Finance, the Comptroller, and a Senior Financial Officer. This went well.

The second day on location at the client's head office, however, Nathan and Jeff faced the first challenge. It was the practice for a tea trolley to be pushed around the client's office in the afternoon from which office workers, (those with white skin) were offered tea and a biscuit. These were real crockery cups and dishes and therein *lay the rub*! Jeff came to Nathan and asked him if he should avail himself of this service.

"Jeff, you are a full member of this audit team, so join with us and come grab a cup of tea," Nathan said confidentially.

Off they went. The next day the Comptroller reported confidentially to Nathan that the visit to the tea trolly had raised some eyebrows and generated a few complaints. Nathan and the Comptroller agreed that this was the first test and they must uphold the decision to allow Jeff to participate in the afternoon tea, along with all other office workers. That was Round #1.

Round #2: Nathan gave Jeff an audit program covering the company's export register which a Mrs Van der Merwe maintained manually. This employee was what the audit team referred to as a *verkrampte.* A *verkrampte* in the days of apartheid referred to an Afrikaner Nationalist who was against any changes in the government's apartheid policy. This would be the kindest way to characterize such a person. In any case, when Jeff presented himself to this bookkeeper, she refused to allow Jeff to access her register! Nathan immediately went to the Comptroller and this was sorted out quickly. Mrs Van der Merwe had to eat some humble pie and allow Jeff to audit her register.

Round #3: Nathan and Jeff were at one of the company's recording studios where certain toilets were clearly labelled WHITES ONLY. All black personnel, including musicians, technicians, and others had access to a toilet which was reached from the outside of the building. Jeff came to Nathan with a question:

"Nathan, which WC should I use?"

Nathan pondered this one for a moment. This was trickier. Nathan had no problem with this himself, but he worried about how the client's employees would react. Without much hesitation, though, he said, "Jeff, you are on our team. You can use the upstairs toilet facility."

Jeff paused for a moment and obviously appreciated being supported by Nathan. He turned to Nathan and said, "Nathan, I am not here to change the world – just to get my Chartered Accountancy designation. While I really do appreciate your vote of confidence, I will use the outside venue."

Nathan internally breathed a sigh of relief, and commented, "It is your decision Jeff."

After these incidents, the ground rules were effectively established and from then on it was business as usual. Nathan was very pleased that Rob Potts had backed him up all the way.

Nathan had another unusual experience while working in Johannesburg. He discovered that there was an ice hockey league in existence in the city consisting of four teams – an Austrian, a Swiss, a Canadian and a South African team. Before he knew it, Nathan had his skates shipped out and he was playing on the Canadian side – the *Jungle Jets*. To top things off, the players shared in the gate revenues, so Nathan made the equivalent of Can$50 per game for doing something he loved to do! The team had an Asian trainer, Pritam, who was

Indo-South African. He and Nathan spoke often and over time it became clear that Pritam and his family longed to live in Canada. Before one game, Nathan brought Pritam some information about Canada, and its immigration policies. Pritam expressed his thanks and asked if Nathan and his wife Julia would come to his home to meet his wife and family and have dinner. Pritam and his family lived in Lenasia, at that time a segregated Indian township next to Soweto.

Nathan was not sure whether it was against government policy for him to visit Lenasia, but nonetheless he accepted the invitation. At nighttime with no street lighting it was almost impossible to locate Pritam's house. Finally, he and Julia located the very modest residence where they met the family and enjoyed a delicious Indian curry meal. Imagine the reaction from Nathan's maid and gardener a few months later when Pritam and his wife joined Nathan and Julia for dinner at their home! This kind of mixing was unheard of in those days in South Africa; but Nathan was just a naïve Canuck!

Nathan tried on a few occasions to organize a job offer for Pritam in Canada, to no avail. Thereafter, he often wondered if Pritam and his family ever made it to Canada. He hoped they did because they would have become great Canadians citizens.

Chapter 12

Ça continue

Jacques had willingly agreed to write a letter to the Chief of Police in Sault, Édouard Mercier, requesting a copy of the accident report that covered the motor vehicle crash that occurred on May 19 and took the life of his dear brother, Serge. Writing this letter was required before proceeding to the next step which involved appealing to *La Commission d'Accès aux Documents Administratifs* (the *Commission for Access to Administrative Documents)* should the request for the information be formally denied. As Nathan and Jacques had discovered earlier, this Commission is an independent administrative authority that oversees and interprets access to information laws in France.

Jacques had sent the letter by registered mail and a few days later he had received a reply.

"Well, the letter from the Sault Police Chief has arrived," Jacques alerted Nathan.

"Oh, well what did he say?"

"No big surprise. He declined to share the report with me – and by extension with you and Pierre."

"Did he provide any reason or rationale?"

"Not really. It was a very bare-boned attempt at justification. I will fax or e-mail his letter to you and Pierre. He just said that under French law, he was not required to provide this type of information, and that doing so would compromise privacy rights and would work against the national interest. Fin. End of story!"

"Ha, ha," laughed Nathan, "we will now proceed to the next step. If you go to the web site of the Commission, you will be directed to a Referral Form or Formulaire de saisine. It is a fairly straight forward form that needs to be completed, following which the form can be sent electronically to la Commission. I think this form should be completed by yourself, if you don't mind, given your more direct connection to Serge."

"Yes, not a problem. I haven't had a chance to look at the Commission's web site or read the form. What kind of information are they looking for?" Jacques enquired.

"They ask for your coordinates; the administration concerned, in this case the Sault Police Municipale; the object of the request and what the request relates to, in this case the fatal motor vehicle accident on May 19 where your brother was killed; and, documents subject to the referral. In this case we do not have any documents, and we are seeking a copy of the accident report. Perhaps you could attach a copy of the report in the Marseille newspaper, La Provence. I will e-mail a copy to you or send you the link if needed."

Nathan continued, "You are then asked to submit a copy of your letter of request to Chief Mercier for the information; together with the reply from the Sault Police Municipale. There is an area at the foot of the form entitled Observation. It would be my view that in this area you should build a compelling case why you would like an official report on the circumstances surrounding your beloved brother's accident and death. He is your only brother, you are in Paris, etc. That's about it."

"Great," said Jacques. "This doesn't sound too onerous. I will get onto it right away. What I would like to do, if you agree, is to send you and Pierre a copy of my response in draft form for your review and comment. I would feel better doing it this way because I get the feeling that both of you are more experienced in these matters. Is that OK?"

"Absolutely. Send us a copy when you are ready," confirmed Nathan.

"À la prochaine," concluded Jacques.

"Mais oui. I will call Pierre and fill him in on our discussion today and we will both look out for the Referral Form in due course. Merci Beaucoup," Nathan ended.

Chapter 13

Il se souviens

Two days after Jacques and Nathan had spoken on the telephone, Nathan and Pierre received a faxed copy of the Commission Referral Form that Jacques had drafted. The three of them were all in agreement that the form hung together well and that a good case had been made to be granted access to the accident report. Jacques had subsequently transferred the form electronically to the Commission. Now it was a matter of waiting for a response. It was not known how long it would take for the Commission to answer, and their web site provided no clues.

Nathan was surprised that the Sault Police Chief, Édouard Mercier, had refused to provide a copy of the accident report. The privacy argument didn't seem to hold water – after all, Serge was dead. Likewise, claims of threats to national security seemed particularly bogus. Hopefully the Commission would overrule the Captain and they would see the Accident Report.

Nathan was certainly no expert in police matters, but in his earlier life he had served once as a security officer and later as a quasi-police officer. These were both summer jobs while attending university and, in neither case, did Nathan's responsibilities involve filling out detailed incident reports!

His first summer job leading up to his freshman year in university, at the age of sixteen, was as a security officer aboard a river cruise ship. The river was the Saguenay in the Province of Québec, and the ship's name was the *SS* Richelieu. Weekly voyages started in Montreal and visited *Québec* City, Murray Bay (La Malbaie – Pointe-au-Pic), Tadoussac, and finally Chicoutimi at the head of the Saguenay River – and then back again to Montreal.

Most of the passengers on board were Americans coming to experience the beauty of the area and the unique and charming Québec hospitality. Nathan wore an officer's uniform and ate in the Petty Officer's Mess. This mess served up meals including, amongst other things, the ends of sliced tomatoes, birthday cakes with misspelled icing inscriptions, and day-old cinnamon buns. The word Officer was a euphemism – not so the word Petty! The security officers worked eight hours on, eight hours off. Their job was to conduct regular tours of the ship looking for fires, excessively rowdy behavior, and vandalism.

At the start of his shift, Nathan would report to the bridge and check in with the senior officer there – typically the second or third mate. A Watch clock system was employed on his regular patrols. Watch clocks were located around the ship in pre-determined locations.

Nathan had a key which activated the clock to indicate that he had checked the area in question. Once clicked, a light would show up on a panel in the bridge area. All lights had to be on when Nathan returned to the bridge. Any stations not lit would be noted by the bridge officer, and the security officer would be required to return to that area and click the watch clock. Missing a clock was unusual once the patrol was done a few times – it was always the same route.

Mixing with passengers was prohibited for crew members. During off-hours, however, members of the crew could head up to the sun deck on a warm day to an area reserved for the crew. Nathan, and his newly-acquired bellhop friend (equally non-status crew member who carried bags, cleaned rooms, and ran errands), Tom Burns, would use these opportunities to bend the rules somewhat and speak with young passenger lasses seated in lounge chairs across the delineated crew/passenger lines. Nathan remembers one occasion in particular.

He and Tom arranged from the sun deck to meet two passengers – sisters from Tennessee – once they were docked in Tadoussac. A meeting point was agreed upon near the main hotel and some distance from the ship. From there they walked down a lonely road to a small lake where they perched themselves on big rocks and dangled their feet in the water. Nighttime quickly came upon them and after some good conversation, some *kissy-face* and intermittent light/medium petting, headlights were noticed coming towards them from the roadway. The two couples scrambled quickly only to hear the voice of the Third Mate and the sisters' father yelling,

"Get in this car immediately," they shouted.

There was absolute silence in the car all the way back to the cruise ship. Once there, the father and his daughters disappeared quickly. That left the Third mate and Tom and Nathan standing at the entrance to the gangplank.

"You both know the rules and you broke them. I am leaving both of you here in Tadoussac. You can make your way home any way you wish at your expense," the Third Mate said angrily.

This was an ugly situation for both Tom and Nathan. Tadoussac was off the beaten track and not an easy place to get to or from. Besides, the whole point of this summer job was to save some money for upcoming university fees.

"Please sir, do not leave us here. We apologize profusely for not adhering to the rules and it will never happen again," they begged.

Fortunately, after more discussion the Officer relented and Tom and Nathan re-boarded the ship.

After that, they were much more careful. Nathan, however, met a charming and beautiful young woman from Grosse Pointe, Michigan, on the sun deck one day. The chemistry between them was incredibly good and before the cruise ended they had swapped photos and corresponded for a few years thereafter. Nathan wanted to go and visit her in the USA, but for a variety of reasons it never happened.

Nathan's other quasi-police job developed a few years later. Uncharacteristically, he had not lined up a summer job in his finishing year at university. Off he went to the Canadian Pacific Railway staffing office located in Windsor Station in Montreal. His timing was perfect and he was in luck and hired as a Police Constable in the private CPR Police Force. He was fingerprinted and his training consisted of a few gunshots with his assigned revolver into a target in the basement of Windsor Station. He was assigned to work at the CPR marine sheds in the Montreal Harbour. At that time, CPR owned and operated the passenger liners, *Empress of Britain, Empress of England* and *Empress of Canada, and t*he cargo carrying *Beaverboats – Beaverelm, Beaverash, and Beaverpine.* All these ships docked at the CPR shed in Montreal and the CPR police were deployed to provide security and policing in this area.

On Nathan's first day at the docks he realized why he had been hired on such short notice. The longshoremen and stevedores working at the CPR sheds were on strike. They were a scary group – Nathan was told some seventy per cent of the longshoremen had criminal records – as they picketed in front of the sheds.

These were the days before containerization. Pilferage was rampant and hard to stop, even with cleverly designed patrols and enforcement. On one occasion, Nathan recalled, a ship load of French wines arrived on board one of the Beaver ships, for offloading in Montreal. Three CPR constables were assigned to oversee the unloading of this precious cargo. Without the police officers knowing, the longshoremen unloading this shipment constructed an igloo type structure from the wine boxes, with one of them sitting inside the temporary dwelling without being noticed, spelling each other off, and ripping open a box of wine and imbibing on a few bottles! It was only after the shift ended that this was detected, together with the realization that thirty-six bottles of great French wine had been consumed on a four-hour shift.

Nathan thought of many other stories, but his mind kept shifting back to Northern Provence and his dealings with the police there.

Chapter 14

BINGO

Two weeks had passed since Jacques had submitted the Referral Form, or Appeal, to the Commission. Nathan began to wonder when they might hear back with a decision. His thought-process must have been prescient as the phone rang.

"Bonjours Nathan. Ici Jacques," Jacques began.

"Oui, allô Jacques. It is good to hear from you. Comment *ça va?*"

"I am doing well and I am calling you specifically to tell you that we have a decision from La Commission d'Accès aux Documents Administratifs. It is good news, I should add. The Commission supports our position about being able to access the accident report covering Serge's fatality. They have instructed the Chief of Police in Sault, Captain Édouard Mercier, to release a copy of the report forthwith to me," Jacques reported happily.

"That is great news. Well done Jacques."

"There is one more piece of good news. Captain Mercier has already sent me a copy of the accident report by courier. I have only recently read through the report and will get a copy to you and Pierre, one way or another, in the next day or two."

"Any surprises jump out at you in the report?" queried Nathan.

"Yes, a couple of things did get my attention. Firstly, the report was very short and did not contain much more information than Constable Henri Paquette provided us with three weeks ago. The report describes the date and time of the accident, where the accident happened, the driving conditions at the time, the circumstances surrounding the incident; meaning Serge apparently missing a turn in the road, running into a tree and suffering fatal head injuries. The report confirms that speed, alcohol, or drugs were not factors in the accident. As a basis for this last conclusion the accident report includes the results of blood tests administered to Serge. There are three photos which surprised me. I was expecting many more. Perhaps I have been watching too many crime TV series but police seem to take a myriad of pictures at crime scenes – perhaps fewer are taken at the scenes of auto accidents. But for example, I would have expected to see photos of the road where Serge presumably skidded off and left skid marks. Another thing, I could see no evidence of national security issues that were alluded to by Captain Édouard Mercier. Anyway, those were my initial impressions; but there is more," commented Jacques.

"OK. I look forward to seeing the report but tell me more!" Nathan asked.

"On the day that the accident report arrived at my home from Sault, I had a call that evening from a junior Constable, Claude Laurin, working at the Sault Police Municipale detachment. He was calling from his home and sounded very nervous. He told me he was present, together with Constable Paquette, at the scene of the accident. He told me that what he was about to tell me was outside of his job description and the information was sensitive. He could lose his job if I was not discreet. I reassured him that I would treat the information he was about to share with me with absolute discretion. He told me he saw the accident report that was being sent to me the day before and this caused him some concern."

"Wow. Go on," said Nathan

"When Constable Laurin read the accident report he told me that he was amazed that there was no mention of a piece of evidence that was discovered at the scene of the accident. He described it as a nearly complete right forward fender and headlight assembly. He couldn't tell what make of car the fender came from, but it was a dark grey in colour. This evidence was bagged and is sitting in the evidence room at the police station. The other missing piece of the accident report, according to Constable Laurin, is a variety of photos, taken at the accident site. He is not sure what photos are missing. At least fifteen to twenty photos would have been taken by Constable Paquette which would be typical for an accident like this – and only three were included in the report. Besides, Constable Laurin told me he saw many photos scattered on Paquette's desk right after they reported back to the detachment. Laurin couldn't be more specific because at the accident scene he was instructed by Constable Paquette to knock on the doors of the four homes in the vicinity of the accident to ascertain whether or not they had heard or seen anything. He was doing this for some of the time when they were on site. The population near the roadside where the accident occurred is quite sparse. It took him some time to cover all four homes down long driveways, etc. and when he returned to the scene of the accident, things were being wrapped up."

"This is very curious and troubling. Did Constable Laurin question Constable Paquette about these anomalies?" questioned Nathan.

"Yes, he did. As the accident report was being prepared for transmittal to Jacques, Laurin approached Paquette and raised these issues. Constable Paquette told him that Chief Édouard Mercier, told him that the fender located at the scene was already previously there, and had been dumped there by someone there much earlier on a garbage disposal mission. The fender had nothing to do with the accident involving Serge according to the Chief, and therefore did not need to be included in this accident report. With respect to the photos, the Chief had given instructions for the accident report that was being transmitted to be brief and to-the-point and extraneous photos or information excluded. According to the Chief, only a few key photos would be forwarded to Jacques in Paris. The transmittal letter for the accident report was under the signature of Chief Mercier, so the end result was that he called the shots!"

"Good work Jacques. This is a lot to digest but it has a smell to it. I will read the report when it arrives but it seems to me from what you have said, and what Constable Laurin has told you, that we may need to contract with a private investigator to dig deeper into this. The challenge is that you are in Paris, I live in Toronto, and Pierre has kindly agreed to get involved, but he is in Avignon. It seems to me that we need someone on the ground – someone with some law enforcement experience and good contacts. Do you agree, Jacques?" Nathan asked.

"Absolutely, I couldn't agree more. Serge is, and was, my brother so I am happy to pick up the tab for any fees. Do you have anyone in mind?"

"Not now, but I will speak with Pierre in Avignon and we can do some collective research on this. Any ideas you may have would be useful as well."

"Sounds good. Shall we speak again in a few days?"

"D'accord, agreed," concluded Nathan.

"Bye."

Chapter 15

Private Eye

Nathan picked up the phone to call Pierre in Avignon.

"Hello Pierre. How goes the battle?" Nathan posed.

"I am very well, merci. Et tu?"

"Well thanks. I just got off the 'phone with Jacques in Paris so I thought I would de-brief with you and ask for your assistance with something."

"Absolutely, happy to assist."

"Thank you. I feel badly roping you into this matter, but I do appreciate your cooperation and assistance."

"As they say, this is a good cause, and besides, you are a good friend."

Nathan began the de-brief. "Well, there is some good news and some bad news. First some good news – the Commission ruled in our favour and they called upon the Sault Municipal Police to provide Jacques with a copy of the accident report. Adding to that, Jacques has already received the report and he is sending you and me a copy forthwith."

"Good news," commented Pierre enthusiastically.

"Yes, it is. There are some pieces to the news however, that raise flags. The accident report did not add much to what we had already been told. Jacques noticed that there were only three photographs of the accident scene, and he was expecting more. I agree with that assessment."

Nathan continued, "Now, here is the real surprising part. Jacques received a call from a junior constable working in the Sault Police detachment. He was quite nervous according to Jacques, and he indicated that he was not authorized to place the call – but rather he was doing it as a matter of conscience and doing the right thing. Here is what gave rise to this Constable's consternation. This young Constable Laurin attended at the motor vehicle accident together with Constable Paquette and when he saw that accident report that was being sent to Jacques, a couple of things jumped out for him. First, he was aware that several photos were taken at the scene of the accident, probably fifteen to twenty, and he noticed that only three were included in the report. Also, and perhaps more importantly, Constable Laurin told Jacques that in the accident report there was no mention of a piece of evidence – a right fender and headlight assembly – that was not mentioned in the report. This item is currently in a large bag in the evidence room at the Sault Police Department. When Laurin questioned Chief Mercier on both these anomalies, he provided Laurin with what seemed to be half-baked responses. It seems to me that there might be 'Something rotten in the state of Denmark' and I am not sure we will get the clarification and answers we need from Chief Mercier."

"Well, not a pretty picture indeed. Do you think we need to have an independent investigation conducted?" asked Pierre.

"This is precisely what Jacques and I spoke about. He agreed to cover the cost of a private investigator if we proceeded in that way."

"Well there are surely many private investigators in France, keeping an eye on straying spouses if nothing else!" commented Pierre.

"Yes, exactly. When you receive the copy of the accident report from Jacques and you have read through it, if that, together with what we have just discussed, leads you to conclude we should hire an investigator, could you try and locate a good one in Provence. If you could come up with a short-list, perhaps you, Jacques and I could have a conference call and select the right candidate. If you think we should go in another direction, in other words not hiring an investigator, let me know."

"Yes, for sure. I will check out the local scene here in Avignon and in Aix en Provence, and let you know what I come up with. From time-to-time such firms are advertised locally. I will also make some discreet enquiries with some local friends of mine. They might have some ideas. Private investigators are sometimes mentioned in the media in connection with crimes solved. It seems to me that someone with experience with the Police Nationale would be an asset and more inclined to an independent view of the work of the local municipal police unit in Sault. Someone also with good contacts and relationships in the surrounding area would, it seems to me, be a great benefit," commented Pierre.

"Absolutely. Nous sommes sur la même page, as they say! Let's leave it at that for now, but before you go I should give you an update on what Fairmont Hotels and Resorts is up to. Not much to report except to say that they are still interested and evaluating the business case. I spoke recently with Fairmont's Vice-President of Business Development, Cameron Sutton, and he told me that he and a small team flew to Provence recently to survey the landscape – not in a legal sense but in a visual way – and they came away reasonably happy. We will just have to stay in touch with them and see where it goes. Anything else to report at your end?"

"I am glad you asked," Pierre began, "because I should tell you about a town hall meeting, or stakeholder consultation session, that was conducted by HELIVOL recently in Avignon. HELIVOL has conducted a few of these consultation meetings in the last few weeks in Aix, Sault and Apt; but this is the first one I was able to get to. The purpose of these meetings is of course for HELIVOL to make the local population feel more comfortable with their proposal for low-level helicopter test flights. I attended, as did several people from the protest group that Serge led – complete with HELIVOL-NON placards. Others in the group have stepped into a leadership role in Serge's absence, which is great. The session began with introductory comments from Alain

Pelletier, the Canadian President of HELIVOL. People listened but you could hear a pin drop when he concluded his remarks. A PowerPoint presentation followed from Pelletier's underlings and that was not enthusiastically received either. Pelletier wrapped up the meeting after taking a few questions and a few boos. At one point he turned quite aggressive and made some insulting remarks about what he referred to as the socialist's view of development. This did not win him any friends. Anyway, that was that. The meeting ended and everyone went home, many mumbling as they went."

"Well done. Thanks for that important bit of info. Shall we leave it at that for now? I will look out for your call when you are ready."

They exchanged goodbyes and signed off.

Chapter 16

Stories

Nathan and his wife Erika lived in the Kingsway, on the west side of the City of Toronto. The Kingsway was a quiet residential area not far from Lake Ontario or downtown. Nathan had built a good life for himself and his family. They had one unmarried son living and working in Ottawa. Later in his career, Nathan had started a boutique consulting firm focused on promoting good governance and combatting corruption. The firm's clients included governments and industry sectors and companies committed to improving their performance in these areas. Of course, corruption comprised a supply and demand side – the payers of bribes and those who take bribes. Nathan and his colleagues focused on what they referred to as *grand corruption*, or *big-ticket* corruption, in contrast with petty bribery.

It was a warm week-end evening in Toronto and a perfect time for a back-garden bar-b-que with close friends. Nathan's business partner, Mike, and his charming wife Isabel had joined them for drinks and dinner.

Over drinks, while Isabel and Erika pondered Canadian politics, and the upcoming Toronto International Film Festival, Nathan and Mike caught up on a few matters.

"Mike, how was your recent trip to Tanzania?" Nathan asked.

"Well, the workshop with Parliamentarians went very well, but the logistics of getting there and back were brutal," Mike responded.

"Oh, how so?"

"Getting to their nation's capital, Dodoma, took me thirty hours from start to finish. Next time I will clearly break up the trip with an overnight stop in Frankfurt, but this time, naively, I flew direct. I say direct, but the itinerary was Toronto to Frankfurt, Frankfurt to Addis Ababa, Ethiopia, and then Addis to Dar es Salaam. That is where the fun began! Tanzania's national capital used to be in Dar, but by 1996 the capital had been moved inland to Dodoma – four hundred-and-fifty miles due west. They are currently building a commercial airport in Dodoma, but right now there is a landing strip only – which is good if you have your own plane or charter aircraft! A young chap driving a Land Cruiser picked me up at my hotel in Dar es Salaam and we drove like crazy over eight hours to reach Dodoma. We must have passed thirty trucks on this two-lane highway – all of them transporting goods to either Dodoma or to the turnoff to Arusha. I must say, he was a good driver, but there were some hair-raising moments! I stayed at the New

Dodoma Hotel which was an interesting experience. On our way back I commented to the young driver that if that was the New Dodoma, I would shudder to see the *Old* Dodoma! He got a good laugh from this and took it in his stride which kept us entertained on the drive back to Dar."

"Wow, what an exhausting experience," observed Nathan.

"Having said all that, the anti-corruption workshop went well and as it turned out the timing was perfect. The workshop was held on a Friday all day, and a half day on Saturday. On the Thursday prior to this weekend, Tanzania's Minister of Finance had tabled a budget which meant that the budget debate would occur the following week. All of the MPs wanted to stick around for that – besides they were all somewhat locked into Dodoma given the location of the capital in the middle of nowhere – so we had about seventy-five MPs in attendance – a very good turn out. They are all very committed and engaged which made the sessions very productive. Tanzania clearly is a corrupt country. Sadly, last year, in the 1998 *Corruptions Perception Index* prepared by Transparency International, Tanzania ranked eighty-first out of 85 countries with a score of 1.9 out of 10, when 10 is considered corrupt-free, if that were possible! We approached this assignment in the usual way. In advance of the sessions, we developed a *gap analysis* to identify the major holes in the governance model for Tanzania – in the context of corruption. At the workshop, since we were working with Members of the National Assembly, we identified where MPs could exert the most influence to effect positive change. From that, a three-year action plan was developed. So, we will see where it goes from here. At the conclusion of our sessions, the Speaker of the National Assembly told me she was very pleased with the process and the outcome – so that is a good thing. So, what is new in your world?" concluded Mike.

"Before I get into that, just a quick story about an experience of mine in Arusha, Tanzania, a few years ago. I was there for meetings and staying at a local hotel. One night, around three in the morning, my hotel room phone rang."

"One of my colleagues said, 'Nathan, you should come down to the lobby right away – there is a fire in the hotel.' I turned on the light next to my bed and low and behold my room was filled with smoke. Down I went to a packed lobby where I was told that a fire had broken out in the kitchen and the smoke had been sucked into the ventilation system throughout the hotel. Firefighters had put out the fire, but the smoke was everywhere. Fire alarms had worked in some of the hotel rooms, but not in others apparently, because I hadn't heard anything. Perhaps it was a question of how deeply one slept, and how loud the alarm signal was – who knows. Well, we couldn't go back to our hotel rooms so we sat in the hotel lobby for a couple of hours until the smoke cleared in our rooms. The next day I spoke to the hotel manager and told him he should check out the alarm system. In this instance there were no injuries or casualties, but they may not be quite so lucky next time if the alarms didn't work properly. Anyway, that is my story," ended Nathan.

Nathan continued, "Well, seeing that I am in the process of lightening up my workload, by way of contrast, I feel I have been standing still listening to your work in Tanzania! A couple of things come to mind, though," Nathan offered.

"Great – fire away, no pun intended!"

"Sure. At a seminar I attended recently I was impressed by a presentation made by a representative from the *Maritime Anti-Corruption Network (MACN).* The MACN is using its global power, one hundred members globally, to take collective action in the fight against corruption."

"Companies engaged in shipping goods containers, oil, and other commodities throughout the world by sea, began to realize that they were all, in many ports, facing the same extortion demands, and requests for bribes, before their ships could be off-loaded. An example was cited. In one particular port a ship would dock, an official would board, ask for the paperwork, and would re-appear some time later stating that the forms were incorrectly completed, and that a $20,000 fine had been levied. These allegations by the port authority officials were contrived and false."

"These MACN companies got together and they completed a company-by-company anonymous survey asking, by port, what their experiences had been. From this survey summary they identified the most problematic ports which they then visited with a delegation from MACN. Firstly, they outlined their collective corporate market power. They then indicated that if these extortion and bribery requests did not stop, vessels would stop at other ports, or bypass that country completely. Apparently these interventions have had the desired affect and the results have been very positive," Nathan continued.

"It got me thinking about how this collective action by MACN could be replicated for global industry at large. Companies operating multi-nationally are frequently exposed to the dilemma of asserting their strong corporate ethics policies when their competition has no such constraints. Hence – the uneven playing field."

"I have approached The Business Industry Advisory Council to the OECD which is well situated to examine the feasibility of such an industry-wide approach, and ultimately to recommend collective action to OECD members if merited. I have encouraged them to meet with representatives of the MACN and explore their business model and its possible applicability more broadly. I am hoping this initiative has some legs. I will be following-up with BIAC shortly," Nathan told Mike.

"Sounds promising. Anything else cooking?" Mike enquired.

"A few other business irons in the fire, but on a more personal level I have become involved with a two other friends in France – one in Provence and the other in Paris – in trying to figure out whether or not there is a business opportunity for some new upscale health spas in Northern Provence. This follows Erika and my visit there last year, when we met an engaging fellow – who regrettably lost his life in a car accident just a couple of months ago. His brother in Paris, together with a friend of mine who lives part time in Avignon, are involved in trying to sort that out as well. I won't bore you with all the details, but it is taking up some of my time."

Nathan continued, "One last thing. I spoke on the telephone yesterday with our mutual colleague, and corruption crime fighter, Rodney Barker. He was in Washington DC briefly as he is traveling the world on a grant to study the relationships between commercial tax evasion, bribery, money laundering, and economic growth. He is also working on a book about money laundering and illicit financial flows. We three have often wondered out loud why world leaders like Indonesia's President Suharto embezzled $15-$35 billion; Muammar Gaddafi of Libya who is getting close to $20 billion in stolen money; and Hosni Mubarak of Egypt well on the way to illegally stashing away some $70 billion, are continuing to accumulate more wealth than they can ever use? Rodney offered what, in my opinion, is a plausible explanation. It is his view that after a certain point the corruption has very little to do with the money, and more about proving that he or she is shrewder, smarter, and has more street smarts than those around him. It also becomes addictive – the power and the control and the feeling of dominance. This all makes sense to me and helps to solve the puzzle that has perplexed me for many years now."

Nathan finally sat back and laughed.

"That's about it. We are getting far too serious. Why don't we join the ladies and I will get the bar-b-que going so we can eat tonight!"

Chapter 17

Vive le Québec!

Pierre and Nathan had met each other for the first time at university and they became good friends. After university their careers took them separate ways – Nathan living and working abroad in Bermuda and South Africa, and Pierre joining the Canadian diplomatic corps in the commercial trade section, representing Canada abroad. Pierre, while playing hockey in France, met Suzanne, the two of them married, and they traveled the world together. When Pierre and Suzanne settled back in Canada, he and some colleagues launched and ran a small investment firm located in Montreal. Pierre had also served on the Board of Directors of VIA Rail Canada, the nation's passenger rail service.

Pierre and Nathan showed a high level of mutual respect, and they got along famously – so well in fact that later on in life Nathan and Julia named their son after Pierre. Pierre came from a very established Canadian family, but one would never know it interacting with

Pierre. Nathan loved that about Pierre and this attitude reinforced their bond.

Pierre retired at an early age and he and Suzanne split their time between Montreal and Avignon. Avignon was a welcome relief from the Montreal winter from March until June with temperatures averaging twelve degrees Celsius. Not balmy, mind you, but better than Montreal at that time of year! Also, there were many things to do in Avignon. In fact, Pierre and Suzanne had recently enjoyed a jazz concert in a park on the outskirts of Avignon.

Pierre and Nathan had many experiences together, but two events stuck in Pierre's memory. The first was on November 22, 1963 – the day when President John F. Kennedy was assassinated. Pierre and Nathan were driving in Pierre's car with two other friends from the Eastern Townships to Montreal when this horrific tragedy was announced on the car radio. The four of them were shocked and numbed. Pierre pulled the car off the road and they listened intently for some time before moving on. It is amazing how so many people remember where they were, and what they were doing, on that day.

The other memorable situation was when Pierre, during university days, invited Nathan and two other friends to Quebec City in February 1963 to experience the Québec Winter Carnival. They all stayed at Pierre's sprawling family home in Québec City. They had a tremendous time and Pierre appeared to be very happy to have hosted the group. How well Pierre remembers the group singing repeatedly the Carnaval refrain –

Carnaval, Mardi gras, Carnaval
À Québec c'est tout un festival
Carnaval, Mardi gras, Carnaval
Chantons tous le joyeux Carnaval.....

Pierre had been convinced that his visitors particularly enjoyed the ice canoe race across the St. Lawrence River where forty plus teams compete, fighting the powerful current, the very cold weather and navigating over large chunks of ice. Often the individual teams had to get out of their boat to by-pass, or push the boat, over the frozen blocks of ice. Pierre and his family had hosted an amazing private reception in the magnificent l'Hôtel Château Frontenac overlooking the River where the boat racing teams were competing. It was quite the day. On other days they visited many interesting spots in the city and participated in some events. They enjoyed the night parades, snow sculptures, and the Bonhomme Carnaval's Ice Palace.

But now Pierre had to focus on the task at hand – to locate a private investigator who could help them get the answers they needed about Serge's death. Pierre knew he would have to deal delicately and discreetly with the search. He didn't want rumours to start circulating that would point fingers back at the Sault Police Municipale.

Pierre approached the task in different streams. He used his local network, engaging with people he could trust and who would treat the matter as confidential. This approach resulted in a couple of good leads. Pierre also browsed the web looking for private investigators in the area and he checked out *les pages jaunes* for any prospects. Not surprisingly, the bulk of the more promising private investigators were located in Aix en Provence, and, to a lesser extent, Avignon. Pierre developed a short-list of five people with phone numbers, and he decided on an approach. He would be very guarded about what he would tell these individuals in the opening salvos in terms of the background to, and mission of, the project. He would start with prospective investigators providing him with a summary of their background and a description of what types of cases they typically worked on. He decided he would be particularly interested in investigators with working experience in the Police Nationale and those whose expertise went well beyond snooping around digging up dirt on marital indiscretions.

Pierre made the calls and had some interesting conversations with those on his list. One individual stood out. His name was Louis Prud'-homme and he was based in Aix en Provence. Pierre set up an appointment to meet the private investigator at a less frequented and more private café located on the famous Le Cours Mirabeau in Aix. Le Cours Mirabeau is a very wide boulevard in Aix covered over almost completely with plane trees and dotted with fountains, and cafés. It is a beautiful and charming place visited by millions and an ideal place for a coffee or lunch.

At the appointed time, after Louis and Pierre had identified each other based on their individual descriptions over the telephone, they sat down at a table in the café. Pierre had arrived early and selected a table which was more conducive to a confidential discussion. Their conversation was conducted in French.

"Bonjour Louis. C'est un plaisir de vous rencontrer," Pierre began.

"Et pour moi aussi," replied Louis.

They both ordered a café au lait.

"I know we spoke on the telephone, but tell me about yourself, Louis," Pierre began.

"Well, I was born and raised in Aix and following École Polytechnique I joined the French Foreign Legion in which I served for fifteen years. Following that I joined the Police Nationale right here in Aix. I retired prematurely so that I could set up my private investigator practice. The work I do is vary varied and covers many different types of operations and scenarios. Discretion and thoroughness are my watchwords. I know many people in this area, both law-abiding and otherwise. With respect to the former, I joined the Rotary Club in Aix some years ago, partially as a business development tool, but also because I believe in the work that Rotary does. In fact, we meet weekly just down the street from here. So, the bottom line is that I am a committed professional with deep roots in this community. I keep focused on a project until a successful conclusion is reached."

"Great, thank you," Pierre commented.

Pierre was feeling extremely comfortable with Louis so he began to describe their team – Jacques in Paris, Nathan in Toronto, and himself in Avignon – how they came together and what their concerns were with respect to Serge's death.

"I agree with you. Something is not right," asserted Louis.

"Louis, can you describe in general terms how you would approach this assignment, based on what I have told you?"

"Well, the first thing to do is to establish the origin and circumstances surrounding the fender assembly. As a working hypothesis, I would assume that the fender is a piece of the puzzle relating to the car accident and Serge's death. One thing for sure, someone would have needed to have a new fender installed on his or her car in a body shop shortly after it went missing, so to speak. So that is where I would start. There are only a certain number of body shops in Northern Provence and most of them are in Aix. I would identify all the shops where the job could have been done – presumably the day following the accident. I would use my network and detective sense to decide on which shops to visit. A body shop would remember replacing a right fender – it's a matter of getting their cooperation in disclosing this information if it happened in their shop. I am confident I can do that. I would also do some discreet snooping around to establish if and why the Sault Municipal Police detachment appears to be tampering with evidence. Taking Constables Paquette or Laurin out for a coffee might be a good place to start, but we would need to think about that and talk it through, as it could be touchy. The process I would use would be iterative – in other words I would follow the information and evidence," Louis concluded.

Louis and Pierre then spoke about a few other project matters relating to Louis' background and tactics.

"Thanks. Your approach sounds to me to be a good one. As mentioned, if we hire you the contract will be with Jacques in Paris, but we will pay your fees from here. I need to ask, what do you charge for fees?"

"Typically, I charge on an hourly basis. It is very difficult to work on a fixed fee or even to give an accurate estimate because it depends on how the information comes together. I will provide you with a weekly report on work completed, results achieved, and the work plan for the next week."

Louis then provided Pierre with his hourly rate and gave a rough estimate of the price range for the completed assignment.

"Fine, that all sounds reasonable. I now need to speak with my partners in this exercise. Just so you know, I am inclined to recommend to them that we engage you, so don't accept any other projects in the next few days. I will get back to you very soon. Does that sound all right?" Pierre asked.

"Yes, perfect. I will await your call. Merci."

Chapter 18

Sounds Fishy

Pierre left Aix feeling very satisfied after his conversation with Louis. He jumped into his car that was parked on a side street off Le Cours Mirabeau and set off towards Avignon. Once home, he sent an e-mail message to Jacques and Pierre suggesting a Skype call for the next day. That day didn't work for Nathan so they agreed to Skype the following day in the afternoon.

This was good news for Pierre because he had planned to do some fishing on Thursday, and now he could. One of the other reasons he loved Avignon was that the area was famous for its fly fishing – and Pierre was a very keen sports fisherman. The other good news was that the grayling fishing season had opened in late May and fishing for trout had started in mid-April.

The River Sorgue runs for thirty-six kilometers between Fontaine de Vaucluse and the Rhone River near Avignon. The fishing spots near Avignon were close to where Pierre lived.

Grayling do well in cold water as Pierre knew well – he had fished for Arctic grayling in the Northwest Territories, north of Yellowknife, and in the Yukon west of Whitehorse and Haines Junction in the Kluane National Park. Grayling are noted for their large sail-like dorsal fin and their spunk, especially in cold water. The waters of the River Sorge are cold by Mediterranean standards so it is an ideal river for trout and grayling fishing, even though the fishing is challenging because the fish do not get fooled easily. Pierre liked the challenge of mixing the flies, the tackle, and the casts – and getting it just right.

Pierre had been fortunate to have sport fished in many parts of Canada, and in other locations – in Bermuda for wahoo and tuna; in Barbados and Hawaii for mahi-mahi and marlin; in New Zealand for rainbow trout and marlin; in Mexico and Costa Rica for snapper and sailfish; and in South Africa for barracuda and bass. Fishing for Pacific salmon off British Columbia, for Chinook and Coho, were real highlights as well.

One trip that he would never forget developed when he was working during the month of September on a management consulting project in Yellowknife, Northwest Territories. Because of the distances involved, he would stay over in Yellowknife for weekends. Such was the case on one occasion when, on the Friday evening he had a call from his work colleague, Gerry, who lived and worked in Yellowknife.

"Hey Pierre, how would you like to do some Arctic Char fishing this weekend? The Char are running in the Tree River and you need to strike when the iron is hot, so to speak. The char move into the rivers from the

Arctic Ocean to spawn this time of year. They spawn, and unlike most Salmon, they return to the ocean after the spawn. There is a charter heading up there for the weekend early tomorrow morning and one of the participants has cancelled. They offered his spot to me, but I have something else on this weekend. Are you interested?" Gerry asked.

"Are you kidding? Of course I would love to go. I don't have a fishing license, any fishing gear, tackle, warm clothing or waders. Also, what is the price?"

"Not a problem, the guide will write up a license for you – about twenty bucks I believe – and you can borrow my rods and tackle. I have some very warm clothing for you and chest waders that you could use as well. The price for the gear is zero of course but the Charter company dings you for four hundred dollars," Gerry replied.

Pierre recalled, The Tree River flows into the Coronation Gulf, an arm of the Arctic Ocean. It is east of Coppermine and six hundred kilometers north of Yellowknife; interestingly far north of the tree line so how is was named the Tree River is anyone's guess!

"OK, I'm in," Pierre confirmed.

"I will let them know. The Twin Otter float plane leaves from the dock tomorrow morning at 5 a.m. I will show you where you have to go early tomorrow. I should tell you, if you are not there before 5 a.m. they will leave without you, so set your alarm!" Gerry added.

The balance of the Friday evening could have been characterized as organized confusion. Gerry was amazingly helpful digging out the tackle and gear and briefing Pierre on how it all worked.

"The plane will land on the ice on a lake about halfway up to the Tree River to re-fuel. It is a Cariboo hunter's station. The next stop is the Tree River which is very narrow, but you will land there just off the Coronation Gulf and the pilot will beach the aircraft on the pontoons onto the riverbank. Your group will divide up and fish all day Saturday, and into early Sunday afternoon," Gerry advised.

"Sounds good."

"Now one word of warning as I have done this before. After fishing all day Saturday, a huge bon fire will be started, obviously from firewood brought up from Yellowknife. There will be lots of toasting with Scotch and beer. By the way you need to take your own booze. Then around midnight the pilot will propose a poker game inside the plane."

"So, what are the stakes?" asked Pierre.

Gerry passed along this information, which lead Pierre to conclude that he would probably skip the poker game.

The take-off from Yellowknife, and the landing on the Tree River some time later, went as planned. After exiting the plane, the group scattered along the riverbank and began fishing in earnest. Many Arctic char were caught. Much of the fishing was catch-and-release as one could take only two fish back to Yellowknife. After a great day of sunshine and exercise, sitting around the campfire that evening quaffing an ale and eating Arctic char cooked over the fire, together with some rolls, was a gastronomic delight. Sure enough, around midnight some of the group, including the pilot, headed down to the plane for a game of poker. Pierre retired to his pup tent and slept like a log that night. The next morning the chatter in the camp was that the card game had gone on until 4 a.m. The pilot and others had drained a bottle of Scotch and then some. The pilot had lost some $1,400, and he was flying the group out later that day, Sunday, sometime after mid-day depending on the weather! They were also being told, in addition to gutting the fish they were taking back with them, that they should remove the heads and tails. In other words, weight was an issue – and looking around at the other fishers Pierre was not surprised. Taking off from the Tree River later that day and negotiating three bends in the river before they cleared land, was a numbing experience for Pierre – but they made it. In true fashion, Gerry kindly smoked one of the Arctic Char, and deep froze the other for Pierre. Pierre, Suzanne and their friends had a real feast later back in Montreal.

Pierre also thoroughly enjoyed his annual trip to Labrador to fly fish for speckled trout. For these one-week outings, Pierre, his dear friend Dave, George, and two others flew to Goose Bay where they overnighted at Hotel North after shopping for food, drinks, and fishing tackle. The next morning, they boarded a float plane, and flew over the Mealy Mountains to the Eagle River. The outfitter camp they stayed at was privately owned by Dave and others and was located upriver at the headwaters of the Eagle River, where the speckled trout thrived. At the river mouth, some one hundred and eighty kilometers downriver and north east from the camp, fishers try their luck fly fishing for Atlantic Salmon. Because of the remoteness of the camp where Pierre and the group fished, the speckled trout grew to six pounds. Northern Pike were also featured for a change-of-pace, and typically grew to twelve to fifteen pounds.

After a full day of fishing, often including a shore lunch of fried trout cooked in traditional Newfoundland and Labrador *salted pork rinds, or scrunchions,* the group would have a full dinner, clean up and then retire to the screened-in porch looking over the river, where stories would be told over single malt whiskeys and Cuban cigars. Great memories, but Pierre was very saddened when his good friend Dave died; and Pierre's motivation to return to the Eagle River diminished.

But now, Pierre had to prepare for his fishing venture the next day. Maybe the fishing gods would be with him.

Chapter 19

Love hockey

As Pierre awoke the next morning, he reflected on the results of his fishing exploits the previous day. One small trout, and one grayling in his creel – not a bad catch. He had done worse. Grayling do not keep very well exposed to the elements, so the idea is to cook them soon after they are caught. This Pierre and Suzanne had done for dinner, coupled with some tasty roasted veggies and a bottle of Rosé wine.

As he rolled over, he felt aroused. He touched Suzanne who was just waking also, and she signaled her interest. Both of them often had sexual urges in the morning so they were very compatible that way as well. In an instant they were engaged in passionate love-making – a great way to start the day Pierre thought. They showered together afterwards and resumed where they had just left off in bed. They toweled off and headed to the kitchen for breakfast.

They enjoyed the usual breakfast fare, café au lait and almond croissants.

Suzanne was a very interesting person, as was the way that Pierre and Suzanne met. She was born and raised in Grenoble, France – in fact just over two hundred kilometers from Avignon. She had enjoyed the 1968 Winter Olympics in her hometown, especially the performance, and good looks, of the Frenchman Jean-Claude Killy who won the three alpine events at the '68 Olympic Games. Later, Pierre would recall how he had been cheering for the Canadian, Nancy Greene (Raine), when she won a gold medal in the giant slalom, by one of the largest margins in Olympic history, and a silver medal in the slalom.

Pierre went to McGill University in Montreal for his post-graduate degree, and this is where his athletic prowess really surfaced. He was Captain of both the McGill Redmen varsity football and hockey teams. After graduating he was approached by an alumni friend, Ted, who had played, as a professional, for the town hockey team in Villard-de-Lans, France. The town is slightly less than forty kilometers south of Grenoble. Ted told Pierre over a beer at a local Montreal pub what an amazing experience it had been. The standard of hockey in the league in which they played was a level or two below that of the semi-pro teams in North America – so you could be a star player – notwithstanding one's relatively modest credentials in Canada. Pierre decided to take the plunge. Ted undertook to call the team manager in Villard-de-Lans to recommend Pierre for the team. Pierre then followed-up with the team manager in Villard-de-Lans using the coordinates provided by Ted. The manager was very enthusiastic and invited Pierre to join the team as both player and coach. Pierre was thrilled and started packing his bags. The team covered his travel costs to and from France, and his accommodation once in Villard-de-Lans. The pay was less than startling, but the team schedule took them throughout Europe, a region that Pierre to that point had not fully experienced, and one that he was keen to explore. Once there and playing/coaching he realized there were other perks. As a local hero, perhaps undeserved, he had to fight off, depending on his mood and the occasion, the groveling fans and groupies. He lost some of his innocence during that winter in France!

Suzanne had traveled down from Grenoble one afternoon to Villard-de-Lans with a girlfriend to watch the local hockey team play a visiting team from Belgium. Watching Pierre coach the team, while playing a great game of hockey at the same time, convinced her that this was the man for her. It was love at first sight. At a reception for both teams after the game she assertively walked over to Pierre and introduced herself. And the rest as they say is history. They married soon afterwards.

Firmly back in Avignon, Pierre completed a few chores around the house and garage, and readied himself for the 2 p.m. Skype call. He was reminded that while Erika and he were visiting Estonia a while back, he became aware that an Estonian, Jana Tallinn, together with two other countrymen, had played a key role in the development of Skype. The audio call was scheduled to accommodate Nathan in Toronto with the six-hour time difference. When it was 2 p.m. in France, it was 8 a.m.

Daylight Saving Time in Toronto. Nathan was an early riser so he would surface at 6 a.m., shower, shave, dress, and grab some breakfast in time for the Skype call.

"Bonjours," they echoed.

After comparing the weather in their respective jurisdictions, Pierre kicked off the discussion.

"I should probably lead off. I checked out a number of sources to come up with a private investigator that we would all be comfortable with, and I believe I found our man."

"Good news. Tell us more," Nathan and Jacques blurted out simultaneously.

"Louis Prud'-homme comes highly recommended by many in my network. He lives in Aix and was born and raised there. Following École Polytechnique he served in the French Foreign Legion for fifteen years. He then joined the Police Nationale in Aix from which he retired early so that he could become a private investigator. The type of work he does now is varied and diverse and goes well beyond spying for married couples. He is very well connected in the community, through Rotary, his law enforcement background, and via his involvement with many people and activities in the community," Pierre paused.

"Sounds good so far," the two others chimed in.

"I asked Louis how he would approach this assignment, based on what I had told him. I liked his response."

Pierre then proceeded to tell the group how Louis would approach the investigation. He highlighted the fact that when Louis was with the Police Nationale in Aix he dealt with many of the body shop owners, in different capacities, and in fact he directed some business their way from time-to-time.

"Louis believes that using his network and calling upon his diplomacy and discretion, he will be able to locate the body shop that replaced the fender they seek."

"I think you have found a good one Pierre. Well done," said Nathan.

"Do you agree, Jacques?"

"Absolument," chirped in Jacques from Paris.

Pierre continued, "Great. But he doesn't come cheap."

Pierre then described the price quotes that Louis had provided to him. "He would like to bill weekly, based on his weekly report to us, and plan for the next week."

"I think we should go for it," Jacques said.

"I agree," confirmed Nathan.

Jacques continued, "Pierre, would you confirm these arrangements with Louis and sort out some of the logistics for us? We will need a contract between myself and Louis. There are some options as to how I could pay Louis once the three of us are happy with his weekly bill. I could make a direct deposit to his bank account if he is willing. Otherwise, I could mail him a cheque or money order. There may be other ways of doing this, like e-banking. Pierre, could you handle these modalities?"

"Yes, not a problem. I will contact Louis later today and lock this up. I will ask him for a work plan for the coming week, and we can go from there," concluded Pierre.

"Bon, une réunion productive," offered Jacques.

"Nous sommes d'accord," said Nathan in agreement.

"Jusqu'à la prochaine fois," they all asserted.

Chapter 20

Sea bass

Jacques looked out of the window of his apartment in Saint-Germain-des-Prés in the 6th arrondissement of Paris, France. It was a beautiful day and he was looking forward to taking a stroll along the Seine later. Another favourite area where Jacques liked to spend some time was le Jardin du Luxembourg which was quite close by, also in the 6th arrondissement. He could sit there for hours and watch all the people stroll by. It also attracted interesting buskers from time-to-time, as well as musicians who would play in the bandshell. There was always a quiet corner as well. Paris was rich in museums and galleries and two of Jacques favourites were the Musée Dorsay, and the Musée Rodin, both not far away in the 7th arrondissement. But it was the cafés and the restaurants that truly made Paris different and special. Of course, the famous Café de Flore, a favourite haunt of Jean-Paul Sartre and Simone de Beauvoir, the philosophers and existentialists through the 1900's, was close to where Jacques lived and he could often be seen there.

Pierre had e-mailed to Jacques a draft contract between the private investigator, Louis, and himself, to review and sign. Pierre also messaged that Louis would prefer that fees and any expenses be deposited directly into his bank account in Aix. He had provided Jacques with the bank account details. This arrangement suited Jacques since he felt somewhat like *roadkill on the information highway* and he had not yet entered the world of e-banking. The contract looked fine. Jacques had added a clause that stipulated that Louis would be paid a bonus, at Jacques' discretion, if Louis came up with the information the group was seeking. Pierre thought this was a great idea and it had been incorporated.

Jacques had lost his wife, Émilie, to cancer two years ago; and now his only brother Serge was gone as well. He was determined to get to the truth about Serge's death. Jacques and Émilie had had a great, albeit somewhat short, life together. Jacques was now retired and occupied himself with a paint brush and canvass – sketching and painting scenes and people in and around Paris. In the final years of Jacque's career, he worked as a senior sales and marketing executive with a large French pharmaceutical company. He and his wife had traveled the world before her premature death, but one trip kept re-surfacing in Jacque's memory – a trip to Italy five years earlier.

Jacque's boss, the President of the company, was married to a woman with expensive tastes and a particular love of Tuscany, Italy. She had convinced her husband that the company needed a villa in Italy that could be used to entertain customers and major suppliers. After a search by a real estate agent on their behalf they located an amazing property with magnificent views of the rugged shoreline and crashing waves on Monte Argentario, on the coast of Tuscany not far from the town of Grosseto. A two-laned scary road along the cliffs connected this villa to the small quaint fishing village of Porto Santo Stefano. The area suited their snob instincts because in times past, and to some extent still, celebrities, wealthy Italians, and other so-called *beautiful people,* could be seen in cliff-side villas there. As an added advantage the villa was ninety minutes from Rome, within two hours of Siena and Florence and under one hour from the Tuscan vineyards.

Naturally, the villa was acquired in the name of the company, but instead of hosting customers and suppliers, it became a favourite haunt of the President and his wife, and other senior company executives. At some point Jacques was asked if he and his wife would like to spend two weeks at the villa. He jumped at the opportunity and a plan was put in place. Another plus – the villa had a local hospitality worker who cooked the meals if asked and kept the house clean. To give the appearance that this was a business trip and to be fully expensed, a dinner meeting for Jacques with the company's senior salesman in Rome was organized for the end of their Italian tour.

Once ensconced in their villa, they decided to venture down to the fishing village, Porto Santo Stefano, to buy some local fish for dinner that evening. When they arrived at the port, they noticed that the fishing boats had just returned from the sea. Porto Santo Stefano was very Italian, with hardly another European, North American or Asian in sight. Jacques stepped up to one of the vendors' stalls and pointed to a group of fish on ice. He decided to speak in broken English and so, in his best Anglo-Italian, he posed the question.

"What kinda fish isa dat?"

"Sea bass," was the expressive reply with arms wailing.

On to another stall some steps away they went and Jacques pointed to a very different type of fish.

"What kinda fish isa dat?" Jacques repeated.

"Sea bass," again another vendor responded.

This experience was repeated several times, at different stalls and for very different fish varieties. Jacques and Émilie had a big laugh over this and concluded that perhaps sea bass was the only word the locals knew in English to describe a fish – any kind of fish! In any case they finally bought some fish and enjoyed their seafood meal later that day back at the villa.

After ten joyous days sitting in the sun, reading, and enjoying meals accompanied by a glass of fine wine, they headed off in their rented car towards Sienna and Florence. In Sienna they enjoyed a wonderful lunch on an outside table in the famous Piazza del Campo. Their visit came in-between the running of the renowned horse races in the square – maybe something for a return visit another time. They carried on to Florence where they were enchanted with the wonders of the Uffizi Gallery, and later the Galleria dell 'Accademia' where the original statue of Michelangelo's famous David, is housed. What history and culture!

After a couple of days in Florence they headed to Rome. Getting to their hotel while navigating the various ring roads around Rome was a challenge, but they finally found themselves in the lobby of the hotel where they were staying. Dinner with the company representative had been arranged for 8 p.m. and Jacques and Émilie were running late so an efficient check-in was on their radar. Initially, to Jacque's disgust, the hotel clerk could find no record of their reservation. Jacques pulled out a written confirmation and handed it across the counter.

"Here is the problem," the clerk asserted, "this confirmation is from head office."

Jacques was astounded. Why was a head office confirmation not applicable he wondered in amazement? Nonetheless, after a few mild threats, an upgraded room was found for them where they headed to shower and change after a long day on the road.

The company's senior salesman, Antonio, was sitting in his car when Jacques and Émilie exited the hotel. After friendly introductions, Antonio asked, "I wasn't sure what type of cuisine you preferred so I made two reservations – one at a very fine restaurant featuring local Italian fare; and the other at a very popular seafood restaurant. Which one would you prefer?"

"Let's go to the seafood restaurant and on the way there I will tell you why," Jacques responded.

On the way to the restaurant, Antonio heard the sea bass story. They all laughed uproariously.

At the sophisticated seafood restaurant they were greeted by a very welcoming maître d'hôtel with a white towel hanging on his arm, to be escorted to their table.

On the way, they passed a beautifully presented array of seafood displayed on ice on a long table along a wall.

Jacques stopped, pointed at a fish, and enquired of the maître D, "What variety of fish is that one?"

Without hesitation, the Maître D answered, "Sea bass."

Jacques and Émilie looked at each other and then at Antonio. Antonio, having just guffawed at the sea bass story, turned beet red with embarrassment. Jacques turned to Antonio and they both had a laugh.

After being seated, a waiter appeared, and after a pre-dinner drink, he returned to take their order. Antonio spoke to him in Italian for what seemed like an eternity. He then told Jacques and Émilie what he had done which was to ask the waiter to bring a variety of different fish to the table, in a sequence, that the three of them could share with accompanying vegetables. With each fish brought to the table the waiter would describe the fish, its name and origin, which Antonio would translate as best he could into English.

The meal was delicious, they learned much about the local fish populations, and a good time was had by all. Jacques, however, never looked at a menu the same way, particularly if sea bass was featured!

To top the trip off, they had a weird experience with the rental car in Rome. The day before Jacques and Émilie were flying from Rome to Paris, he checked his wallet.

"I have a pile of lira that I should get rid of. I noticed that the car we rented in Paris before we left, from European Car Rental, has a drop-off facility just around the corner from here. I should return the car here in downtown Rome and pay the bill with these liras. We will then take a taxi to the airport tomorrow morning. Sound good?" he asked.

"Good to me," replied Émilie.

The next day, as planned, Jacques drove the car around the corner, checked in the rental car, and paid with lira bills.

One year later, back in Paris, Jacques had a telephone call.

"Hello. I am with European Car Rental. I am checking to ensure that you checked in the car that you rented from us last year in Italy."

"Yes, of course I did. That was one year ago! In fact, I kept the paperwork in a file in my home here – bit of a pack rat you know! I will fax to you the final bill and the payment acknowledgement signed by one of your company representatives in Rome," Jacques promised.

"That would be most helpful. Thank you very much and goodbye. I am sorry for having disturbed you," the car rental employee said as he signed off.

The company was never heard from again. Jacques speculated that the company representative who checked in his rental car pocketed the lira and never recorded that the car had, indeed, been returned. The employee probably ran off with the car as well. Que sera sera.

Chapter 21

Slave trade

Nathan was reading a great novel, by a Victoria, B.C. author, Esi Edugyan, entitled *Washington Black*. It is a story cast in the 1830's about a field slave, *Washington Black*, who works on a Barbados sugar plantation. He makes an escape with the help of his master. Although offering no real or valid comparison, Nathan's mind turned to a demanding summer job of his.

After graduating from university with his undergraduate degree, Nathan, like so many others, faced a mountain of student debt. Nathan and his good friends Desmond, and two brothers James and Richard, headed out to the Province of Alberta at the end of their final university term to earn some fast money for their bankers. The previous summer James and Richard had worked as labourers on the Great Slave Lake Railway which ran from Pine Point, Northwest Territories, to Peace River, Alberta. They had earned good money, albeit in difficult conditions. Nathan and Desmond were motivated by the lucrative pay and a desire to continue onto graduate studies at the end of the summer.

The Pine Point Mine produced lead and zinc ores between 1964 and 1988. The town of Pine Point in the Northwest Territories was built by the mining company, Cominco, and when the mine closed the town was abandoned and demolished. The Great Slave Lake Railway was built and operated by Canadian National Railways. The ore was loaded onto ore cars in Pine Point to reach its first destination in Peace River, Alberta. From there it went by rail to a Cominco smelter in Trail, British Columbia. The railway was built on permafrost (muskeg) which greatly increased the challenges of laying the track; and once operational, to detect movement of the roadbed and tracks and thereby avoid derailments. The management had obviously decided that the economic imperatives of moving the ore before the track had settled took precedence over the occasional minor derailment. Trains traveled very slowly and minor derailments were corrected relatively quickly by dispatching a locomotive from Peace River with a mechanism to pull the ore train back onto the tracks. Canadian National Railways out-sourced the recruitment and management of the labour crews to a human resources company.

The four students were keen as they flew out to Edmonton, Alberta where, as impoverished students, they stayed at the Salvation Army Hostel for a few days before heading up to Peace River. The labour crews (gangs as they were then called) came in two varieties – section gangs and extra gangs. Section gangs patrolled certain sections of the track on what the workers called putt-putt cars, or railway motor cars, and made every effort to re-align railway tracks, and buttress the roadbed with gravel – all to avoid derailments. The extra gangs, by way of contrast, traveled the length of the railway buttressing the roadbed with extra gravel.

The four students were hired almost instantly in Peace River and sent to join their work gang. Nathan initially was separated from the three others to work on an extra gang close to the Alberta/Northwest Territories border. Two weeks later, he re-joined the others on an extra gang at a time when the crew was just heading north on the line from Peace River. The section gang work was less demanding, but more isolated and lonelier, but the physical demands of the work on the extra gang were significant. They worked seven days each week all summer, for fourteen to sixteen hours each day. Desmond had the good fortune to be chosen by the foreman to work in the dining car kitchen, where he peeled vegetables and washed dishes on parallel shifts every day of the week. The other three students envied Desmond. Oh, to be peeling vegetables and washing dishes every day in lieu of shovelling gravel! There was nothing else to do that far north anyway; but still the work was very repetitive – shovelling gravel onto the railway tracks all day – and very tiring.

In the mid 1960's, there was no minimum wage in the Province of Alberta so labourers on the railway were paid $1.50 per hour! However, on Saturday workers were paid time and one half; on Sunday the pay was double time for all hours worked, and any hours worked on weekdays over ten hours was also paid at time and one half. It is easy to see how paychecks soared given the number of hours worked. They were each charged $2.50 per day for room and board. Nathan and his friends left Alberta richer by about three thousand dollars each, which, by any reasonable standard was a good haul for a student summer job in the 1960's.

The extra gang workers lived in rail cars attached to other cars including a dining car, an administration car, and others. The cars were coupled together and were parked on railway sidings alongside the main line. Periodically a locomotive would appear and move the staff train farther north as the gravel work was completed. Their foreman, Bill Chapwya, told them his goal was to complete one mile each day. He worked them hard to achieve that – often even begrudging them a ladle-full of water working under the scorching hot sun. Many of the other workers came from Portugal or Italy. Typically they were working on temporary work visas with the hope of staying on through the winter, since section gangs were needed year-round, and eventually becoming permanent residents in Canada and bringing over their families to join them. Sometimes the gangs were joined by workers from Edmonton, but they often lasted only a few days.

One of the Portuguese workers, John, was the author of some discord within the extra gang. He was lazy which meant that one or more of the other workers had to pick up his slack. When you are working fifteen-hour days shoveling gravel, picking up someone's slack because they are lazy, is not tolerated. John was also first into the dining car after each shift and always picked a spot right next to the kitchen door. When the cook's helper came into the dining car with a plateful of food, John would grab it and almost demolish the contents before any of the other labourers had a chance to have any. The rest of them had to wait for the next plate. Needless to say, after a long hard day of work, these were not popular moves. They would often call John out on this rudeness, but their protests fell upon deaf ears. Every now and then, the four college students would speak to the Portuguese elders, and John's Portuguese co-workers would take John into the bush and, as they described it, *put the shovels to him.* This would improve his behavior for a week or so, but he would revert to his normal routines until the next time.

During the entire summer, their group escaped the camp once for a dinner at a restaurant in a very small town – High Level, Alberta. In the mid 1960's the town consisted of a grocery store, a post office, a beer parlour and a restaurant. Nathan, Desmond, James, and Richard hitched a ride into High Level with the timekeeper, who kept a car on site and parked it next to the siding they were on at the time. The trip required meticulous planning! They would arrive back in camp after their shift on the put-put car around 9 p.m. after working all day, wash their faces and maybe change clothes, and then race off in the car to the beer parlour and restaurant. It was a very rushed affair given that they surfaced the next morning at 5 a.m. for the next workday; however, this change of routine was very energizing.

Their foreman was a somewhat older man, and seemingly eccentric. They discovered that he was a member of a Masonic Lodge when he pulled the four of them aside, itself an extraordinary down-time event, and posed this question. "Did you know that a Mason has never been hanged in Canada?" he asked.

The four of them were embarrassed by the fact that this amazing historical phenomenon had escaped all of them!

In any case, it was back to current reality. Nathan was looking forward to the conference call the next day with Louis – when Pierre, Jacques and he would be updated on Louis's endeavours.

Chapter 22

Body shops

The Skype call was booked as a video connection so that Jacques and Nathan could meet Louis person-to-person, in a manner of speaking, for the first time. Louis had acquired a reasonable fluency in English from his time in the French Foreign Legion and his world travels. He would be speaking in English and reverting to his mother tongue when he hit some lingual turbulence. Nathan had a good working knowledge of French, and of course Jacques and Pierre were bilingual, so it was anticipated that they would all be able to communicate effectively.

"Est-ce-que tout le monde est ici?" queried Jacques.

"Oui....Oui.....Oui.." came the replies.

Introductions were then made and a cordial atmosphere was created. Louis was then asked to brief the group on his progress-to-date.

"Bien sur, J'ai eu une semaine intéressante," Louis began.

The others nodded in agreement, in unison, as if in pre-ordained consensus.

Louis began, "Firstly I should tell you that my working assumption is that the right fender and headlight assembly are somehow connected to Serge's terrible mishap – more than a mishap, his death. That being the case, it would have been evident that someone after 7 pm on May 19 was driving in a car, at or near the site where Serge crashed, and this car was distinguishable by the fact that it was missing a right fender assembly. There were no witnesses to the accident. At that time of day it would have been very difficult, I suspect, to find a car body shop nearby that was open. In fact, based on the other part of my research, I have determined that there are no auto body shops near the accident site. More on that later."

Hearing no comments, he continued, "The police would not be very happy to come across someone driving a vehicle on the highway at close to sunset without a right fender and headlight assembly. This leads me to believe that the driver could have pulled over to the side of the road, or into a side road nearby, and spent the night there. I suspect the owner or driver, for a number of reasons, would be highly motivated to have his or her car repaired as soon as possible. At sunrise the next morning, before there was any traffic, or police on the road, he would have taken the vehicle to a body shop somewhere, The question is where. Any questions or concerns so far?" he asked.

Jacques asked the others if they had any comments or questions, and, hearing none he asked Louis to carry on.

"So the first task was to identify the auto-body shops in the area of Northern Provence. I was actually amazed at how many there are. I could not locate any in Sault and only one in Apt. The logical places to take a car for body work would be either Avignon or Aix en Provence. I located fifteen of them in Avignon and twenty in Aix. I decided to call the body shop in Apt and visit in person the body shops in Avignon and Aix. My view is that it is easier to get people to cooperate if you are there in person. The challenge is to create the circumstances, as best as possible, where the body shop owners or managers will tell you whether or not they replaced a complete right fender and headlight assembly on a car on or around May 19-21. An obvious response could be – 'work that I do in my shop is a confidential matter between me and my customer'. Along similar lines, the body shop personnel could indicate that for reasons of privacy there are not able to comply. To be candid, in many of the interviews I had to deploy all the charm and charisma that is in my body! As you all know I am a local, and known to many, and I know many people here as well, so this made the task easier. In any case, enough about the difficulties and challenges – that is what you are paying me to overcome. Any questions at this point?"

"What kind of reception did you encounter overall?" Jacques asked.

"Well, I am glad you asked. Actualy I have yet to meet or interview all thirty-six garage owners, but I am partly through the list and generally speaking I am getting the kind of information that I need. There have been a couple of exceptions so far from people who are very principled, dogmatic, stubborn or obstinate – or whatever adjective you would like to use."

"Let me tell you how I have been approaching these body shops. My typical introductory lines are 'Good afternoon. My name is Louis Prud'-homme. I am a private investigator, formerly with la Police Nationale. I am representing a gentleman in Paris who lost a brother in a car accident in May. The brother is understandably distraught and on his behalf I am following up on an unexplained piece of evidence that was found at the scene of the accident. The item in question is a complete right fender and headlight assembly, dark grey in colour. My client and I would like to know if you recall replacing such a piece of body work on a car on or about May 19, 20 or 21 this year. I do appreciate that this information may be considered confidential but I ask for your indulgence to help this man get to the truth about the death of his dear brother'."

"That is the jist of what I have been saying. I sometimes vary this introduction depending on the sense I have of the personality of the person on the other end of the line, or if I know the person or know of them through a mutual acquaintance or other way. I need to be flexible in how I begin the conversation and how I deal with the response I get. I have been asked if the police have investigated the matter and I say, yes they have but they don't have answers to the question about the fender assembly."

Louis continued, "In terms of results to date, I called the body shop in Apt and was told in unequivocal terms that that body shop had not recently, or perhaps ever, performed that type of job on their premises."

"In Avignon, I have now met personally with some twelve body shop owners or managers. I have no concrete leads so far but based on the meetings I have had to date my instincts tell me that the body work was not done in these facilities. This coming week I will complete the interviews in Avignon and then begin the process in my hometown, Aix."

"That about wraps it up for now. Any questions or concerns?" Louis concluded.

"I think you are headed in the right direction and I am pleased with the progress so far. Anyone else have any concerns or questions for Louis?" Jacques asked.

Nathan and Pierre both indicated that they were happy with the way the project was proceeding and they looked forward to the next report.

They wrapped up the meeting with, "Bon. À la prochaine."

Chapter 23

Hernando's Hideway

A year earlier, Nathan was attending meetings of the EGMONT Group in Lima, Peru when he was called at his hotel and invited to lunch at the home of Hernando Sotillo in the Miraflores area. The EGMONT Group is an organization made up of the vast majority of financial intelligence units around the world who are devoted to the exchange of expertise and financial intelligence to combat money laundering and terrorist financing.

Nathan was thrilled to be able to spend some time with Hernando, the noted Peruvian economist, who had spent his life fighting to create ways and means for the poor to enter the economic mainstream of societies.

Hernando had tracked Nathan down and had made arrangements to have Nathan picked up at the hotel and delivered to Hernando's beautiful home. They sat on the patio for three hours and covered many topics. Nathan had met Hernando at a small gathering at Grano's Italian Restaurant in Toronto a year earlier, where they had chatted and exchanged business cards. He continued to be impressed with the man's breath of knowledge and insights. An article that Nathan had written recently on the topic of global corruption had caught Hernando's attention and he was anxious to talk.

The work of both Hernando and Nathan had similar objectives – to create opportunities for millions of people to move out of the ranks of the poor. For Nathan it was by significantly reducing grand, or *big ticket*, corruption by world leaders. For Hernando it was to ensure that all people had equal access to secure rights to their real property and business assets. Hernando began in Peru by working with the government and offering the poor in that country an alternative to that proposed by the *Shining Path*, a terrorist group bent on the violent overthrow of the system. Hernando proposed what is referred to as the *Other Path* which called for the reform of the system from within and creating legally recognized property rights for the poor. Hernando's work is recognized as undermining the *Shining Path* guerilla movement. After this initiative and sometime later, Hernando split with the Fujimori government of Peru over allegations, and convictions, relating to the corrupt practices of that government.

Hernando quoted some metrics from the late 1990's that Nathan thought were staggering. Hernando estimated that the total value of the real estate held, but not legally owned by the poor of the Third World and former communist nations, was at least US $9.3 trillion. This is a staggering sum, nearly twice as much as the market capitalization of all the companies listed on 20 of the world's main stock exchanges at that time, including New York, Tokyo, London, Frankfurt, Toronto, Paris, Milan, the NASDAQ and a dozen others. This represents what Hernando referred to as *dead capital*. For example, in Haiti ... 68 per cent of the city dwellers and 97 per cent of people in the countryside are living in housing to which nobody has clear legal title. In Egypt, dead-capital housing is home for 92 per cent of city dwellers and 83 per cent of people in the countryside. Without clear legal title to their dwelling, and no assets to pledge, opportunities to secure a loan to start a new business are limited if not impossible. Micro-credit in some areas is an option, but it is not available everywhere and it is typically tightly rationed.

Traveling around large cities like Cairo, Mexico City, Rio de Janiero, and many others it is impossible not to notice the huge shanty town areas where much, if not all, of the city's labour force lives. Often these homes are made from packaging products and wood and metal scraps. Some have been in the family for many years such that through the informal system their ownership is recognized and respected; however, legal title is a pipe dream. Poor people can't afford to register legally because it takes too much government paperwork, time, and fees. Lose the red tape, Hernando has shown, and the capital of the entrepreneuring lower classes can grow into something positive and productive. They can obtain collateral to secure mortgages and build more productive lives. Another benefit of secure property rights is that women can leave the home to sell goods at the market, for instance, and children can go to school. After Peru implemented Hernando's ideas, school attendance rose by twenty-six per cent.

Hernando and his colleagues work with governments around the world to reform property laws, reduce red tape, and significantly streamline the processes to register property and create legally binding property rights. Heads of state in dozens of countries have invited Hernando to meet with them to discuss how the reforms that they have spearheaded around the world might work in their own countries. In many cases this had led to the launching and implementation of significant reforms.

Nathan and Hernando had a spirited discussion about the work of a French economist, Thomas Piketty. Piketty was researching the historical dynamics of wealth and income. He was examining, amongst other things, wealth and income gaps leading to inequality. It was early days in his research but he was focused on the growing concentration of income and wealth in the hands of a small group of economic elites – the power of compounding interest on capital being but one of the driving forces. Income amd wealth gaps had grown and shrunk over the years – from the time of feudalism in the middle ages, eventaully through to the period of the great depression and the world wars, to today where recent trends indicated that the gaps were increasing. Nathan was intrigued by Piketty's argument that it was folly to assume that fiscal, monetary and taxation policies throughout the world were optimally geared. Why should we accept this hypothesis, he argues? Were the risk/reward incentives that are obviously needed in a capitalist society reasonably balanced to produce reasonable incentives and a semblance of income and wealth equity? Nathan, like others, were witnessing the gaps growing between the rich and the poor in North America and around the world.

Hernando argued that Piketty was ignoring 90% of the world population whose capital is tied up *under the radar* in the informal sector. Nathan empathized and understood this argument but wondered if this just exacerbated the inequities. In any case, the discussion was lively and enjoyable and they parted on very friendly terms.

After that luncheon, Nathan began to ponder the complementarity of Hernando's work, and the area that was Nathan's focus – the fight against corruption and money laundering. There was clearly overlap in the processes surrounding property registration, and in many such cases petty bribery is a contributor. Nathan was convinced that grand corruption was hurting the poor. The World Bank estimates that more than $1 trillion is paid in bribes globally each year. Other estimates are in the range of 4%-5% of world income annually, or $4 trillion. One can only imagine how many schools, hospitals, kilometers of roads, or disease immunizations this amount of money could buy. To Nathan, corruption represented a huge betrayal of a public trust that leads to a loss of faith and confidence in public institutions, and to a rise in populism. Nathan was proud of the work that he and his colleagues had undertaken; like helping to create annual public declarations by public officials of assets and income; like assisting in the launching of beneficial ownership registers; like holding companies to account for paying bribes; like helping countries set up anti-money laundering regimes, and many other initiatives.

Nathan had left Lima with a renewed sense of purpose. He was inspired by Hernando Sotillo.

Chapter 24

If it's Tuesday it must be Belgium

At the end of the second week of Louis' investigation into the accident, he and Pierre spoke on the telephone. Louis told Pierre that he was happy to have the Skype conference call, but there was nothing unusual to report.

"I have completed the contacts in Avignon and I am about half-way through visiting the body shops in Aix. The process is working well but I have no big leads currently. This coming week I will complete the rest of the visits in Aix. At this time, I have tentatively concluded that I will not contact the Sault Municipal Police. I am not sure we will ever need to do this, and I do not wish to betray any confidential undertakings made by Jacques to Constable Laurin. Besides, apart from the possibility of evidence tampering, which is illegal, that evidence bag should remain at the police department for some time. Does any or all of this make sense to you?" Louis queried.

"I concur with all that you have said. I will check with the others today and if you do not hear from me, you can assume that you should continue as you have proposed, and that we will Skype next week," Pierre asserted.

"Bon. À la prochaine." They signed off.

Pierre spoke with both Nathan and Jacques and they both agreed to postpone the Skype call until the following week.

Back in Toronto, Nathan decided to head down to his office, make a few calls, and have lunch with his partner Mike.

At noon, Mike and Nathan headed off to the Roof Top Patio & Lounge at the National Club on Bay Street.

"What's new?" Nathan asked Mike.

"Well in February I had some interesting meetings and travels that I don't think I have had a chance to tell you about."

"I'm all ears!" Nathan offered.

"This was a trip that was part business and part pleasure. My itinerary took me from Toronto to Panama City; then to Bridgetown, Barbados; in between a day trip to Port of Spain, Trinidad; then back to Barbados; and then to Montreal and finally the return trip to Toronto. In Panama the meetings were hosted by the United Nations and in Port of Spain I moderated a panel on anti-money laundering. In Barbados my wife Isabel and I visited with friends there, and the trip to Montreal was to visit my stepmom who has been ill recently and is in the hospital," Mike said.

"Go on," interjected Nathan.

"One of the challenges was that I needed three different sets of clothing for different purposes and in different climates. Business attire was the order of the day for Panama City and Port of Spain. I needed leisure clothes for Barbados, and finally winter clothing for Montreal. I have never had my luggage so tightly packed. The hardest part was fitting in my winter coat and snow boots. Anyway, I survived!" Mike commented.

"I can understand the dilemma. Was there an attempt to charge you for exceeding the luggage allowance?" asked Nathan.

"Well, as you know as members of Air Canada's Million Mile Club we are treated very well. So, no, there were no extra charges. I shouldn't forget to mention to you, however, that while I was sitting in the Maple Leaf lounge in Toronto awaiting my flight to Panama City, I sat opposite a gentleman named Allan. We got chatting and after a while to told me the two of you went to school together. Unfortunately, I didn't catch his last name."

"Was he a tall good-looking guy?" Nathan asked.

"Yes, he was. I also found him somewhat irritating if you don't mind me saying so. He works in the aeronautical industry and was traveling to Sao Paulo."

"I know exactly who this Allan is. We were at high school together and we played hockey on the same team. He is not my favourite person, to put it mildly," Nathan said coldly.

"In any case," Mike continued, "my meetings in Panama City were for the purpose of evaluating progress under the United Nations Convention Against Corruption, affectionately known as the UNCAC. Those in attendance were largely representatives from governments who are signatories to the UNCAC. I was there, with others, promoting language to be included in the closing communiqué that would call on governments world wide to introduce transparent beneficial ownership registers, to make it clear who has the ultimate economic interest in a company or a trust. We achieved some success in having recommendations along these lines incorporated into the concluding conference press release."

"Well done," Nathan commented.

"Thank you. While at these sessions, however, I had the opportunity to meet the head of N.A.T.O.'s Building Integrity Programme, Sarah Pascal, a Canadian. She was moderating a panel on *Governance in the Defence and Security Sectors* in a sidebar session. I will read to you her mission statement right off their web site."

Taking a deep breath, Mike continued, "'The Building Integrity (BI) Programme provides practical tools to help participating countries strengthen integrity, transparency and accountability and reduce the risk of corruption in the defence and security sector. It promotes good practice, processes and methodologies, and provides countries with tailored support to make defence and security institutions more effective'."

Mike paused to let Nathan absorb what he had read.

"Sarah and I got chatting and she indicated she would like to engage our firm, and she asked me for a proposal after March 31st, their fiscal year end. I am working on a draft proposal at this moment."

"Sounds interesting," commented Nathan.

"Yes, it does, and I was planning, with your consent, to write you into the proposal."

"Absolutely!" said Nathan enthusiastically.

"Great. To continue, after these meetings I flew to Barbados where I met up with Isabel who had flown there separately and we stayed with our friends in their beautiful home on top of a hill with amazing views of the ocean, not far from Speightstown, in the northern parish of Saint Peter. We always enjoy our time with Betty and Kevin. The weather was great so we thoroughly enjoyed the beach, some fishing, shopping, the polo grounds, and a local fish fry."

Mike continued, "While in Barbados I had pre-arranged to moderate a panel in Port of Spain, Trinidad and Tobago, so I flew over there the evening before and back the next day. It was a one-hour flight on Caribbean Airlines highlighted by a three-hour delay that was not mentioned when I checked-in – only later at the gate! I was glad to have decided to fly over the day before the panel. This workshop brought together leaders from many of the Caribbean tax havens – jurisdictions like Andorra, the Bahamas, Belize, the British Virgin Islands, and the Cayman Islands. The purpose of the one-day session was to explore new and improved ways in which these countries could discourage the movement of dirty money into their banking systems. One of the panel members was a representative from the local regional style Financial Action Task Force body. I think it was a good productive session overall, with more to be done obviously. The flight back to Bridgetown was on time and uneventful."

"From Barbados we flew into the bitterly cold weather of Montreal where we stayed for three days – mostly visiting my stepmom in the hospital during the day and catching up with friends and family in the evenings. During our stay my stepmom began to show some improvement which was encouraging. All-in-all a very satisfying and productive trip."

"Well done, partner," commented Nathan.

"Isabel and I had hoped to visit friends who work in the Canadian diplomatic corps in Havana, Cuba, but when we checked the connections we discovered that it would involve flying from Bridgetown to Granada to Panama and then to Cuba – about six hours in the air and in airports just to get there – so we contacted them and claimed a *rain check*!"

"Another time! Onwards and upwards," they concluded.

Chapter 25

A lead

Louis, the private investigator, had been making the rounds, first in Avignon and then in Aix en Provence. Body shop owners and managers had generally been cooperative, but none of them had confirmed that they had repaired a car missing a right fender assembly, certainly in the time frame Louis was focused on.

On a rainy Tuesday, Louis drove into the parking lot of a large body shop, *Auto Plus*, on the outskirts of Aix. The company name sounded familiar to Louis but he couldn't make any connection. He parked his car in the lot and walked into the reception area where he asked to speak with the manager. As soon as Arthur Petit came around the corner Louis recognized him.

"Arthur, bonjours. It has been a while," greeted Louis.

"Mais oui Louis. Great to see you. I left our Rotary club a few years ago and haven't seen you since then," Arthur replied.

"Business has been good?" Louis enquired.

"Yes, very good, Merci."

"Arthur, I need your help," Louis said.

Louis then described his role as a private investigator and the background to Serge's death in the car accident and his connection with Serge's brother Jacques. He told Arthur what he was looking for.

"My client and I would like to know if you recall replacing a complete right fender and headlight assembly, dark grey in colour, on a car on or about May 19, 20 or 21 of this year. This fender was found at the scene of the accident and is largely unexplained. I do appreciate that this information may be considered confidential but I ask for your indulgence to help Serge's brother Jacques get to the truth about the death of his dear brother," Louis asked.

Arthur paused for a moment.

"Louis, I would be happy to discuss this with you but right now I am completely tied up with two customers. Could we do this another time, perhaps over a coffee at a nearby café," Arthur asked.

"Absolument."

They made arrangements to meet the next morning at 7:30 am at a café around the corner from Arthur's body shop.

"À demain!" they chorused.

The following morning, they seated themselves at a corner table in the café.

"Thanks for doing this," Louis began.

"Pas de problème. I wanted to meet off-site to speak about this because I do have some information for you but, as you have noted, services provided to customers are considered confidential and I do respect that. On the other hand, if any information I can provide to you will assist your investigation I feel compelled to cooperate. Also, I know you are a person of integrity and that you will treat what I tell you with absolute discretion," Arthur responded.

"Arthur, you have my complete commitment to act responsibly in these matters, and to respect your position," Louis asserted.

"Good. Well, I do recall – and I confirmed by checking back on our work orders after you left the shop yesterday – replacing a dark grey complete right fender and headlight assembly on a late model Peugeot. It is not easy to forget such a job because it is not often that a complete fender is missing!" Arthur said.

Arthur continued, "When I arrived at the body shop the morning of May 20 at 8:30 a.m. the Peugeot was already sitting in our parking lot. Sitting in the car was a dishevelled man looking tired and distressed. I went up to the car and he rolled down the window. I recognized the person in the driver's seat. It is someone you know as well."

"OK, who might this be?" questioned Louis.

"None other than Maurice Bourque," Arthur replied.

Louis knew Maurice Bourque. He was a known criminal based in Aix with whom Louis had many run-ins when he served on the Police Nationale.

"Mon dieu. How about that. I know Bourke well – too well. I believe he just finished serving some time in Baumettes Penitentiary in Marseille for armed robbery. He was released just a few months ago. Am I right?" Louis asked.

"Yes, that's correct. I was shocked to see him and the state he was in. He acted very nervously and told me he was involved in a minor car accident and that he had lost his fender. There were also scrapes along the entire right side of the car. I asked him if he had reported the accident to the police or to his insurance company and he told me he hadn't. His story was that this was a simple 'fender-bender' and he wasn't reporting it to his insurance company or they would increase his insurance premium. He said that he called the police and was told that they do not involve themselves in minor accidents like this. In any case, Maurice asked me to do the body work, we did up the paperwork, and he left on foot."

"Do you have an address for him?" Louis asked.

"Yes, it is on the work order and invoice and I wrote it down on this slip of paper which you can have."

"Merci. Do you mind if I go and see him?"

"That is fine if you must. Keep my name out of it if you can," Arthur requested.

"Thank you. I will do my best and report back to you as soon as I can just so that we can close the loop on this."

"OK. Bonne chance. I hope we can stay in touch more often now that we have reconnected," Arthur said.

"Yes, I would like that too. We live in the same town so this is definitely doable."

Louis picked up the tab, and they parted.

Chapter 26

Taking over

Nathan was enjoying his morning coffee while he read the Globe & Mail morning newspaper. This was his favourite time of the day, except for the headline in today's Business Section. He turned to his wife Erika.

"I can't believe it! Another major Canadian company is being gobbled-up by a foreign company," Nathan reported angrily.

"Did you get up on the wrong side of the bed this morning?" Erika quizzed, recognizing the irony of this question since as man and wife they slept together every night – Erika on the left, and Nathan on the right.

"Ha! That's a good one. You know I have been lobbying the Canadian government for legislative changes in this area for some time," Nathan retorted.

The newspaper reported that the third largest US forest products company, Weyerhaeuser Co., would be acquiring the Canadian forest products company – Canada's largest – MacMillan Bloedel Inc. To Nathan this would be a sad day. The loss of such an iconic Canadian company, with its important linkages to British Columbia and Canada's historical development, was a depressing thought. This takeover was one of many in Canada, some recently transacted by state-owned enterprises owned and controlled by the Peoples Republic of China.

"But isn't it a requirement that the Canadian federal government review and approve a transaction like this before it can proceed?" asked Erika.

"Yes, it is true that large transactions like these need to be approved by the Canadian federal government. The acquiring company under the *Investment Canada Act* is required to demonstrate that the proposed transaction is of net economic benefit to Canada. But, since its enactment in 1985 the application of the *Investment Canada Act* by the Canadian government has become a redundant rubber-stamp process. Not one takeover has been rejected since Investment Canada's inception! It is not evident that any studies have been performed in Canada to determine whether or not the 12,100 foreign takeovers in Canada since 1985 have delivered the net (economic) benefits to Canada that were promised," Nathan responded.

Many in Canada, including Nathan, were concerned about what was being referred to as the 'hollowing out` of corporate Canada.

"Erika, many respected countries have moved beyond the *net economic benefit* test to a *national interest test*. The United Kingdom, Germany, Australia and Japan all review foreign takeovers within the context of the `national interest` or `public interest`. I have argued in various circles, to no avail to date, that a review by Canada's federal cabinet of all major foreign acquisitions, using the *national interest test*, would ensure that major Canadian corporate icons that are key strategic assets would remain in the hands of Canadians and used to advance our national objectives."

"I have been following this question somewhat in the media and aren't there good arguments by many economists, business leaders and free marketeers who commonly argue that the restriction of foreign acquisitions will negatively impact the flow of inbound foreign direct investments?" Erika asked.

"Yes, in a general sense this is true. Unreasonable barriers, burdensome regulations, and red tape can act as a disincentive to companies looking for markets in which to invest. Reasonable safeguards, however, such as a national or strategic interest test, which are already in place in many other G7 countries, have clearly proven not to be an obstacle to investment," Nathan mildly agreed and continued.

"The experience in Australia is a good example to illustrate this point. Australia's investment policy is set by the national Treasurer and administered by the Foreign Investment Review Board. Australia encourages foreign direct investment as a way to build its domestic economy. Let me go get my file on this in my office."

"OK, don't be long. This is heavy-duty stuff to be talking about over breakfast."

"Yes, I apologize but as you know this topic is one of my pet peeves."

Nathan walked over to his home office and returned with his foreign takeovers file.

"Let me read the Australian government's summary of its Foreign Direct Investment, or FDI, policy."

"Here it is," as he read aloud, "'In recognition of the contribution that foreign direct investment has made and continues to make to the development of Australia, the general policy stance is to welcome foreign investment'."

"That is a very positive opening salvo," Erika observed.

"Yes, it is, and furthermore," Nathan continued, "Australia places relatively few conditions on foreign direct investment. Similar to the provisions of the *Investment Canada Act*, most relatively small purchases of land or business interests by foreigners are exempt from any prior notification to the Australian government. If a foreign interest, however, wishes to make a purchase of land or an Australian company over a certain value threshold, then it must report its intention to do so to the Australian government, triggering a government review. This review process, which elicits comments from relevant parties, is intended to ensure that any larger foreign investment in Australia is not contrary to the national interest. Any proposal deemed not to be in the national interest can be blocked. Generally speaking, however, investments under fifty million dollars are not subject to this review process."

"They seem like reasonable thresholds to me, if indeed somewhat low," Erika opined. "But how does one determine what is or is not in the national interest? What criteria is used?" Erika asked.

"Good question. The decision would require some subjectivity. The framework would not be all black and white – there would be some grey areas. The Canadian federal government would need to lay out the national interest test parameters through legislation, regulation and guidelines," Nathan commented.

"Let me read to you how the Government of Australia has begun to put some flesh on the bones of the national interest criteria. Let me read to you paragraph five of the same document I just read from, which elaborates on the notion of investments contrary to the national interest."

He read the pasage to Erika, "'The Government determines what is contrary to the national interest by having regard to the widely held community concerns of Australians. Reflecting community concerns, specific restrictions on foreign investment are in force in more sensitive sectors such as the media and developed residential real estate. The screening process provides a clear and simple mechanism for reviewing the operations of foreign investors in Australia whenever they seek to establish or acquire new business interests or purchase real estate. In this way the Government is able to encourage foreign investors to operate in Australia as good corporate citizens if they wish to extend their activities in Australia'."

"A good start," Erika asserted.

"Yes, one needs more than that, but Australia has had this legislation on its books since 1975, and it has not affected their inbound foreign direct investment in any significant way. Business has not been 'scared off' by this legislation mainly because Australia has been extremely cautious in their application of these powers. In fact, Australia has rarely used this power at all."

Nathan continued, "One high profile case deserves mention – the proposed takeover by Royal Dutch Shell of an Australian energy company, Woodside Petroleum. The ten billion Australian dollar bid was rejected on the grounds that Shell would operate the company as part of its global portfolio and not in the best interests of Australia. At the time, the decision to block this investment was met with concern by the business community. It was suggested that the investment was blocked on political grounds – Woodside was Australia's second largest oil and gas company. The claim of political interference was vehemently denied by the Australian government which maintained that the investment was rejected on purely economic and national interest grounds. Specifically, the Australian government argued that there were insufficient safeguards to ensure that Shell would not favour its own competing oil and gas projects over a development in the Australian offshore. The initial reaction to the rejected investment proposal was immediate. The day the rejection was announced, the Australian dollar lost about one cent against the U.S. dollar and share prices in Woodside plunged. There was also an outcry in the investment community over the message that this rejection sent regarding Australia's openness to foreign direct investment."

"Interesting, but what were the long-term impacts, if any?" queried Erika.

"Another good question, Erika. The impacts were short-lived. The Australian dollar recovered its lost value soon after, and there was no long-term effect on Woodside share prices. There was also no discernible impact on future investment in Australia. FDI inbound flows that followed the rejection were strong, suggesting that there were no lingering effects from the attempted takeover of Woodside by Shell. While the threshold amounts used by Australia may be low by Canadian standards, and the inclusion of greenfield investments perhaps not required in this country, the foreign investment policy in Australia appears to be sound."

"Makes some sense to me," Erika said.

"Even the United States has implemented a national security test. Many other countries have similar criteria. The Russian government was currently considering limits on foreign ownership in thirty-nine strategic areas, including natural resource deposits and biotechnology. In China new regulations allow officials to block foreign acquisitions of Chinese companies if the deal is deemed a danger to economic security. Many US states have laws that restrict hostile takeovers. Given these facts, is it reasonable to expect retaliation from these same jurisdictions if Canada were to implement a similar test for foreign acquisitions?" Nathan posed.

"One would think not, but it would be contentious," Erika responded.

Nathan knew from personal experience that investment reciprocity does not exist in countries like the Peoples Republic of China. In other words, while Chinese state-owned enterprises are scouring the world to buy up iconic companies in foreign countries, especially natural resource companies, it is not possible for a foreigner to purchase an equivalent iconic company in that country. In other words, there is no reciprocity. Nathan fervently believes as a given, as do most people who have been exposed to this, that all state-owned enterprises in the Peoples Republic of China are strictly controlled by the Chinese Communist Party.

"I fully understand," Nathan continued, "that foreign direct investment is an important tool for the creation of wealth and economic prosperity. It can take many forms, from greenfield investment creating new production or service capacity, to minority equity investments, to debt financing, and sale and leaseback. Foreign direct investment often creates jobs in the host country; it can facilitate economic expansion; it can help to create a more competitive business environment; and contribute to productivity-enhancing investment in machinery and equipment. For these and other reasons, most countries are eager to attract foreign direct investment from around the world. At the same time, however, there are concerns raised about some foreign direct investment – especially foreign takeovers which often are no more than paper transactions offering limited synergies but resulting in the loss of Canadian control."

"Are there any foreign takeovers of Canadian companies that are good for Canada?" Erika asked.

"While it is true that many foreign takeovers result in increased investment in the entity by the acquirer, this is not always the case, and many feel uncomfortable with the idea of foreign ownership of a significant share of domestic economic activity. They argue that foreign-controlled enterprises may not always act in the national, or local interest; that profits can be redirected out of the country; and that foreign ownership could have national security implications in cases where products or industries are of strategic importance. These concerns tend to be most pronounced in the energy and natural resources sectors. For the reasons mentioned above, many countries, including Canada, do not offer foreign investors unlimited access to domestic assets; many limit or restrict investment in sectors deemed to be of strategic, or cultural, importance. Canada has such restrictions in the banking, transportation, telecommunications and cultural sectors."

Nathan stopped and looked at Erika who was listening intently.

"It is my view that China is trying to engineer a dominant position in its supply-chain for commodities such as metals, minerals and oil and gas. The Japanese government engineered an oversupply of metallurgical coal in the 1980's to help their steel mills. I believe that China is trying to accomplish the same thing with its *One Belt, One Road* strategy, and likewise in its efforts to take over Canadian iconic natural resource companies. The *One Belt and One Road* initiative, in Nathan's mind, is Beijing's foreign policy play disguised as infrastructure investment. China has been highly successful with this strategy in Africa with infrastructure investment in developing countries by China in exchange for access to important commodities, feeding China's growth. I would be the first to admit that these Japanese and Chinese strategies are very shrewd and smart. The questions that concern me relate to whether or not these strategies make sense for Canada and other countries at the other end of these moves."

"Sounds somewhat conspiratorial if you ask me," Erika offered.

"Well, call it what you like, that is my take on the matter."

Nathan had heard the argument that foreign takeovers of Canadian iconic companies were not a problem because foreign direct investment (FDI) outbound exceeds FDI inbound.

When foreign takeovers are debated in Canada, Nathan was always puzzled by the argument that as long as Canadian companies are investing abroad, there should not be a concern about inbound FDI. For Nathan the question should be asked – what has one to do with the other? Further, if inbound FDI exceeded FDI outbound, would we then have a problem? The appropriate question to be considered in the context of the debate is: should Canada allow its corporate sector to be 'hollowed out' as long as we are investing abroad? Canada has had a positive balance in FDI since 1997 but Canadians are buying smaller, less prominent enterprises from others, while non-Canadians are focused on our national champions.

"You know, Erika, Barbados, Bermuda, and the Cayman Islands are among Canada's top destinations for direct investment. In other words, while our corporate giants and national icons are being snapped up, Canadians are investing in offshore tax havens! Economists have pointed out that Canada's trade and investment market share has been falling, year-after-year, since the end of the 1970`s. I also have concerns about who are promoting takeovers of Canadian companies, and why. Corporate entities concern themselves primarily with shareholder value and directors are duty bound to maximize this shareholder value. A by-product of this is that corporate executives do very well when foreign takeovers are consummated. Recent reports of multi-million and even billion-dollar executive bonuses have flooded the media lately. Are the private interests of corporate directors, executives, and shareholders always aligned with Canada's national interests? In my opinion this is not always the case. Governments must concern themselves with broader issues. For example, when considering a takeover, policy makers must assess not only short-term impacts, but also mid to long term impacts. They must take into account the possibility of the stripping of corporate assets, plant closures, downsizing workforces, and flipping companies for quick profits. Today, investment bankers and private equity players exist with the primary goal of purchasing undervalued companies and maximizing profits. More often than not, their methods include those just mentioned," Nathan concluded.

He stopped and took a breath.

"Sorry for the long-winded explanations but you know how I feel about foreign takeovers."

"I had an inkling before, but this morning it became clearer and I certainly respect your views, as always," asserted Erika.

Nathan had occupied his soap box on these questions on many occasions and had been accused of being a

Canadian economic nationalist. Was that an insult or a compliment? He never knew which.

Eating his breakfast cereal, Nathan turned his mind to Provence, France, and wondered how Louis was making out.

Chapter 27

In a box

On Thursday, the day after Louis had met with Arthur, he knocked on the door of Maurice Bourke's modest home on the outskirts of Aix en Provence.

"Oui, what can I do for you?" Bourke asked grumpily.

"Bonjours, my name is Louis Prud'-homme. You may remember me," Louis said.

"Yea, a cop, un flic," Bourke said irreverently.

"I was, but now I'm a private investigator. Would it be possible to come inside so we could have a conversation?" Louis asked.

"I suppose so. I have no meetings coming up soon! Just kidding," Bourke said as he tried to be funny.

After they sat down Bourke offered Louis a coffee, which he accepted.

"So, what brings you here?" Bourke asked.

"I have a client who is trying to come to grips with a car accident that took the life of his brother. Speaking of which, a rumour has it that you were recently involved in a motor vehicle accident yourself," Louis responded.

"Why is that any business of yours?" Bourke asked.

"Well, I was hoping you could help me out with some details with a narrative or story line that I have developed about the car accident that killed my client's brother. I am very confident about what I have so far. By helping me you could help yourself. You will recall that I used to work on the Police Nationale," Louis answered.

"Fire away."

"Could I ask you a couple of questions first?" Louis asked.

"Sure."

"Where were you on May 19th and 20th last month?"

"I was at home, here," Bourke answered.

"Do you have any witnesses?"

"I don't imagine that I do because I live alone, but I will have to think about it and remind myself," Bourke replied.

"I am told you were missing a complete fender recently. How did that happen?" Louis asked.

"I was involved in fender bender in town."

"Did you hit another car, or some immovable object?"

"Look, I don't have to answer any more questions," Bourke asserted angrily.

"Your choice. Can I tell you my little story?" Louis asked.

"Why not? Pourquoi pas?"

"Well, I believe you were involved in a crash with the car owned by my client's brother on the early evening of May 19 on Highway D-30 between Sault and Simiane la

Rotunde. You left the scene of the accident, but without a right fender and right headlight. You parked on a side road overnight. The next morning you were on the road bright and early at 6:45 a.m. and you drove slowly and carefully to Aix, arriving at about 8:30 am when you went directly to *Auto Plus*, the car body shop. That is where your Peugeot was repaired," Louis said.

"Interesting theory," Bourke said sarcastically.

Louis had much experience in law enforcement and in interviewing suspects, so he played the game of telling the interviewee confidentially that he had already solved the crime.

"Well, my friend, it is very much more than a theory. It is just some of the details that I am working on, nothing of great consequence," said Louis.

"Now look," Louis continued, "I know that you have just done some time at Baumettes in Marseille, and I can't imagine you have any ambitions to go back there," Louis speculated.

"It is a dump. I won't be going back."

"I can help you achieve that goal, but I will need your cooperation. When I head to the Police Nationale with my information, they will be much more accommodating if I tell them that you were helpful. That is how it works," Louis stated.

"You don't have beans for evidence, and I have nothing to hide; but I will need some time to digest this and to think about it."

"That's fair enough. You may wish to speak with a lawyer as well, but that is your business. Shall I come around next week?" Louis asked.

"Sure, fine."

"OK, merci. I will come back next week. How about Wednesday or Thursday?" Louis asked.

"Thursday is best."

"Done."

Chapter 28

Going to the dogs

The Skype call involving Jacques, Pierre, Nathan and Louis was set for Friday at 2 pm, the day after Louis had met with Maurice Bourke.

"Bonjours tout le monde," Jacques welcomed everyone.

The four parties were on-line so after a few hellos, Jacques asked Louis to update the group.

"I am happy to report that his week has been very interesting, and very productive," Louis reported.

"Wow, tell us more," Nathan interjected.

Louis told the group about his visit to the body shop, *Auto Plus*, and the confirmation provided by Arthur Petit of the body work done on a car owned by a known local criminal, Maurice Bourke.

"Sounds very promising," the others chirped in.

"I agree. Arthur had Bourke's address on file, which I promised to use with discretion and to keep his name out of this where possible. I gave Arthur that assurance and popped around to Bourke's home the next day – Thursday," Louis stated.

Louis then briefed the group on the meeting with Bourke. He pointed out that Bourke did not challenge Louis' version of events on the 19th and 20th.

"I think we will make good progress with Bourke. I am meeting him again this coming Thursday. He has a great deal of experience with criminality so he will know that he is looking at some time in prison for at least a charge of leaving the scene of an accident. That would be a minimum. I am sure we can connect the dots between the fender assembly found at the scene of the accident with his car. Depending on the circumstances, and what happened the evening of May 19th there could very well be more serious charges at stake for him. As a known criminal, he will also understand that if he cooperates, the law enforcement and judicial systems will look kindly at this, and be more lenient. Next week with Bourke I will draw on my interview or interrogation experience to try and push Bourke into a corner. We can talk about the results at next week's Skype call," Louis concluded.

"Well done. Bonne chance la semaine prochaine," the other three enthusiastically praised Louis' work to date.

They agreed to Skype the following Friday at the same time.

Jacques and Louis signed off leaving Nathan and Pierre on the line.

"So, I was very encouraged by Louis' report, and you?" Pierre enquired.

"Absolutely," Nathan agreed.

"Changing gears for a moment, if you have the time, what have you been up to lately?" Pierre asked.

"Nothing much right now, but when my partner Mike was telling me about his February exploits in Panama, Barbados, and Montreal, it reminded me about the trip that Erika and I took, this past February as well, to New York City," commented Nathan.

"Tell me about it," Pierre said.

"For several years, Erika and I have watched on television the annual Westminster Kennel Club Dog Show in New York City every February. We have had it on our 'bucket list' to attend in person one year, so this year we decided to do it!" Nathan observed.

"How was it? Did you enjoy it? Were your expectations met?" Pierre asked.

"It was a great experience and it exceeded our expectations. We booked the event through a travel agent that has organized these tours for years, and it showed because everything went ahead with no hitches and with extraordinary efficiency. Firstly, they booked us into a four-star hotel just one and a half blocks from Madison Square Garden, where the best in each of the seven group competitions, and the best in show competitions, are judged on the final two evenings of the dog show. For example, this year the 1999 best in show champion was an eight-year-old Papillon from the Toy group. Secondly, the best in breed competitions are held at Piers 92 & 94, on the Hudson River. The tour company ran shuttle buses all day long for those two days of judging. We were given a complete dog catalogue, with information on all the dogs competing," Nathan pointed out.

"Sounds highly organized and comprehensive. What were the highlights for you?" Pierre asked.

"Erika and I really enjoyed going behind the scenes, into the benching areas, where the dogs are groomed before and after the judging rounds. We were able to talk to breeders and handlers and to pet the dogs, with the owners' permission, and take photos. That part was fascinating. At Pier 94 we also serendipitously sat next to a judge who was resting between programs and we were able to ask her a ton of questions about the judging criteria, what is required to become a judge, and many other details," Nathan said energetically.

"When in New York did you do anything else, or was it the dog show only for you?" Pierre quizzed.

"We did some other stuff. You know in New York City there is just so much to see and do. We went to the Metropolitan Museum of Art, the Frick Collection and we had lunch at the Tavern on the Green in Central Park. We also took the opportunity while there to visit with our friends who live in New Canaan, Connecticut. They also joined us for an opera at the MET. So, all in all, a great week."

"It sure sounds like you had a whale of a time. I must go now. We will be speaking to you next time at our Friday Skype call. Until then, all the best," Pierre concluded and they both signed off.

Chapter 29

Make or break

Walking up to Maurice Bourke's house, Louis pondered how important this session was, and how he would need to draw on his complete inventory of skill sets to achieve the results he wanted today. He knocked on the door and Bourke answered. Louis entered.

"Bonjours," they both uttered simultaneously.

"Maurice, thanks for doing this. Shall we get right into it?" Louis began.

"Mais oui."

"Maurice, what were the circumstances that took you up to the Sault area? We know that you were there because your fender assembly was found at the scene of the accident," said Louis.

"I was visiting friends," came the reply.

"Do these friends live in Sault, or in an area nearby? Have you known them for a long time? Can you give me their names?"

"You wouldn't know them, but I have known them for some time," Maurice responded.

"OK. Tell me about the accident," Louis requested.

"Sure. I was driving from Sault to Simiane la Rotunde in the early evening. There was a car traveling in front of me going at slow speed. At one point I went to pass and when I was just past parallel with the car on my right we came into a slight bend in the road, to the left. At the same time, I saw this car coming straight towards me in the left lane at what seemed to be at high speed. I had to get out of his way, so I veered sharply right and in doing so I bumped heavily into the car I was passing. The bend in the road, together with the heavy hit to his car, caused the driver to run onto the road shoulder. He then careened off the road into a small ditch and then down an embankment. I heard a loud crash," Bourke related.

"What next? You didn't stop? What happened to the car you were heading into?" Louis asked.

"I missed the car coming at me completely and it kept rambling down the highway the other way as though nothing had happened. I stopped at the side of the highway, made a U turn and went back to where the crash had happened. I couldn't really see or hear anything. I panicked and carried on to a lonely side road nearby and parked my car at the side of the road. I sat there for a while and then fell asleep," Bourke related.

"Then what?" Louis asked.

"The next morning, I awoke just before sun-up around 6:30 am, started the car, and drove back to Aix. There were not many people on the road at that time of the day, and fortunately no police. I went to *Auto Plus* because it is just around the corner from where I live. I arrived there around 8:15 and waited in the parking lot until the body shop opened and then requisitioned them to repair my car," Maurice concluded.

"Maurice, when were you released from Baumettes Penitentiary in Marseille this last time?" Louis asked.

"It was in April earlier this year. I forget the exact date, but it was about the middle of the month."

"OK. Now, can I ask you a more personal question?"

"Sure."

"When you were released from prison, did you have any money?"

"Pas une sous – not a franc in my pocket and just a few francs in my bank account," Bourke replied.

"It is very tough coming out of prison with limited or no financial resources and no job. What was your plan moving forward?" Louis asked.

"Well, I was looking around for any menial job – labourer, driver, something like that. There are also some minimal government programs one can access to keep you afloat," Bourke replied.

"Were you having any luck?"

"Not really."

At this point Louis decided to take a gamble. He had often used this ploy and it often had proved to be successful tactic. In this case, Louis had a theory and he wanted to test it. He could think of no good reason why Bourke would travel to Sault. He believed that someone had made it worth his while. He had to lie, but not much of a moral or ethical issue at play when one finds oneself in a den of thieves, Louis rationalized.

"Well, Maurice, how do you then explain a huge deposit that was made into your bank account in late April? A few days ago I took my file on this investigation to my former colleagues at the Police Nationale here in Aix. I described the scenario as I saw it on what happened on May 19th. They believed there was enough evidence, admittedly some of it circumstantial, to seek a warrant to examine your bank account Maurice. A judge agreed and wrote up a warrant for the police to obtain your bank statements. That is when they noticed this large deposit. What say you Mr Bourke?" queried Louis.

"My rights have been violated – that is what I have to say! That money was a bequest arising from the death of a close relative," Bourke stated.

Louis thought to himself. The tactic had worked. No such warrant had been issued.

"Oh, really. What was this person's name?" Louis asked.

A long pregnant pause followed.

"Look Maurice, my considered opinion, and that of the police, is that someone paid you to run Serge Dubois off the road the evening of May 19th," Louis advanced.

Again, silence.

"If you tell us who that was, this will work in your favour when the police eventually lay charges. I can promise you that. Right now you are facing a charge of leaving the scene of an accident. To charge you with murdering Serge, the prosecutors would need to establish intent. Maybe someone contracted with you to scare Serge and something went horribly wrong. Is that the case?" Louis asked.

"Can you give me a minute," Bourke requested.

"Not a problem."

Maurice retreated to his kitchen. A few minutes later he returned.

"OK, I will cooperate. I was paid to scare Serge, but NOT to cause his death. I was desperate for cash to survive and this person came along with a tempting offer that could save my skin. It would have worked out fine until that car came barrelling straight at me on the road to Simiane la Rotunde. I would have nudged Serge over and yelled something at him. But it wasn't to be. The plan failed."

"Thanks. You are being wise. Can you tell me who paid you?"

"I will need to think about that. Give me a few days," Bourke concluded.

Chapter 30

Fees and Competitiveness

Jacques in Paris sent an e-mail to Nathan in Toronto asking him if there was a good time when Jacques could call him on the telephone. A date and time were arranged.

"Hello. This is Nathan speaking."

"Thanks for taking the call Nathan. How are you today?" Jacques asked.

"I am doing well, et vous?"

"Great, thank you. I am encouraged with Louis' reports. It will be interesting to get the next de-brief after Louis' follow-up visit with Bourke," Jacques said.

"Yes, absolutely."

"I am not calling about that project at this time, however. It concerns another matter completely. I hope you don't mind this diversion," Jacques asked.

"Not in the least. I am all ears!" Nathan said.

"Nathan, you are aware that I worked for a large French multi-national pharmaceutical company, Megapharma. I still stay in touch with the group there.

The other day a few of us from the company met for a drink. I told them that I was working on a project with two Canadians which prompted them to tell me something I hadn't heard before. They reminded me that Megapharma has a wholly owned subsidiary in Canada that works very well and is profitable and sound. They would like to grant selected world product mandates to their subsidiary, Megapharma Canada, for product niches where the Canadian company has competitive strengths. The problem is that it takes far too long to get pharmaceutical products to market in Canada. By the time the federal government approvals come through, often two years after our application, Megapharma has lost first mover advantage. The company president is very frustrated."

"Good to hear that the Canadian company is in their good books, but disappointing that Megapharma in Paris is, understandably, reluctant to help it grow with more product mandates. However, I am not surprised. We have a client, a chemical company, with the same problem. They are a wholly-owned subsidiary of a holding company in Europe – in Germany to be exact," commented Nathan.

"Interesting. So, have you identified where the bottlenecks are, and what to do about it?" Jacques asked.

"We believe we know where the problems lie. As Albert Einstein once said, 'If I had an hour to solve a problem, I'd spend fifty-five minutes thinking about the problem and five minutes thinking about solutions.' In this case, however, I don't think the solution is that obvious! Our client, and indeed all companies in the industry across Canada, understand that to get a chemical approved, or in your case a pharmaceutical product, a user fee is appropriate. They do not argue about the appropriateness of user fees for what are referred to as proprietary services. They understand that this is required. What they abhor, however, are fees increasing with no corresponding increase in service or performance. Since fees have been on the rise, in most cases there has been no corresponding improved service or response times. As you may know, in Canada the average has been seven hundred and fifty days for a drug to be approved. In the United States, the corresponding time is five hundred, to five hundred and fifty days."

"In Europe, the time frame is even less," Jacques interjected.

"Correct. These user fees charges, however, are as high or higher in Canada when compared with these jurisdictions. Obviously, if a pharmaceutical product or a chemical is showing signs that it could pose a health or safety issue, the approval process is moved to another track. But in the vast majority of cases, this is not the case."

Nathan continued, "In the USA, the United Kingdom, and Australia user fees are tied in some way to service and performance. In Canada there is no such linkage to performance. In Australia, drug reviews must be completed within legislated time frames or the relevant authority loses up to twenty-five per cent of the user fee. In the USA, written performance goals tied to the fee collecting authority were negotiated with the industry.

The Medicines Control Agency in the United Kingdom sets targets for 'clearance times'. Are you with me up to this point Jacques?" Nathan asked.

"Yes, I am; and I am very pleased that you are so up-to-date on this problem. Now, notwithstanding Einstein, how does one move forward to find a solution? It is a real pity that Canada is losing economic activity, research and development work, and jobs," Jacques asserted.

"I couldn't agree with you more, Jacques. And I am glad you want to move along to potential answers. In fact, we have a strong ally, Elaine Cosgrove, who currently sits as a Member of Parliament in Canada's House of Commons. Her constituency area in Toronto is home to a number of pharmaceutical and chemical companies – both large and small – and she has been getting an earful from them. She sits on the House of Commons Standing Committee on Finance and last year she convinced her colleagues on the Committee to conduct a review of federal government user fees, which they did. The Committee wrote a scathing report about the lack of transparency and accountability surrounding these user fees. The report was tabled in the full House of Commons, but it went nowhere. So, in frustration, she developed a private member's bill that was recently tabled in Parliament. The principles of her bill are very clear, and, if passed will bring more transparency and accountability to the introduction of new user fees, and any proposed fee increases. Fees will be subjected to parliamentary scrutiny and be benchmarked against similar fees in other jurisdictions. They will be performance-based, so if performance targets are not met, fees will be reduced proportionately. We, and industry as a whole here in Canada, are very pleased with the thrust and contents of the bill," Nathan concluded.

"Excuse my ignorance, but what is the process from here on in with private members' bills," Jacques posed.

"You are in good company Jacques. The process to the finish line is very nebulous and opaque. I must say, however, that MP Cosgrove seems to be on top of this and in control. The reality is, though, that the success rate for private members' bills is extremely low. Most of them deal with very simple matters – like declaring June 15th as the *Day of the Horse* – by way of example only. Many of these Bills '*die on the order paper*' because the time allocated by Parliament to debate and process these private members' bills is minimal. Most of the parliamentary agenda is committed to what is called '*government business*'. Many of these bills die before Parliament is dissolved for an election – in which case the process has to be re-started from the beginning!" Nathan asserted.

"What are the chances of this Bill being enacted into law in our lifetimes?"

"Jacques, I would say there is a 50/50 chance given the resolve of Ms Cosgrove's commitment. Her executive assistant is also pushing hard on this and moving the bill forward on the parliamentary agenda very effectively. It involves 'horse trading' with other MPs to leapfrog the bill ahead. So, that's where we are at. I would be happy to keep you posted if you like as the bill moves through the Parliament here in Canada."

"Yes, that would be much appreciated. What sort of timeframe are we looking at to get this bill passed?" Jacques asked.

"It could be up to two years unfortunately Jacques."

"Well, at least there is something in the pipeline. I will tell our company president who will be pleased to learn that at least there is some movement. Perhaps some of the world product mandates can be held off for the time being. Many thanks, Nathan," Jacques said.

"My pleasure. A la prochaine."

Chapter 31

Truth will out

Louis had called Maurice Bourke and they had agreed to meet. Louis knew that soon he would need to report his findings to the Police Nationale, but he wasn't quite ready yet. Once he handed over the file to the police, he would lose control, and he wanted to ensure that the case was airtight before he did that. He realized that he was walking a fine line because he was obliged to report a crime to the police. He was additionally hesitant because of the actions, or inactions, by the Police Municipale in Sault, and he knew from experience that sometimes police, fortunately not often, cover-up for fellow police officers – even from a different force.

As Louis sat down across from Bourke in the living room in the man's home, he was offered a coffee and each had a mug in front of them when Louis began the conversation.

"Maurice, thanks again for agreeing to meet again."

"It's all right. I am used to this sort of thing," Bourke replied.

"So, you told me the last time that you were going to think about what we last discussed. Have you had a chance to do that?" Louis asked.

"Yes, I have. I spoke with my lawyer and he advised against speaking with you further, but he did acknowledge that now was the time to bargain. My lawyer wanted to be here today, but I told him no," Bourke said.

"Good. I think you and I understand each other and the two of us can make this work."

Louis continued, "You told me that someone contracted with you to intimidate Serge. Can you tell me who that was?"

"I will, but first let me give you the background to the story," Maurice said.

"Sure."

"As I told you when I got out of prison I was virtually penniless. I was scouring around looking for some sort of job when there was a knock on the door. I answered and a man introduced himself as Charles Camus – not his real name I could tell – and he asked if he could come in. He told me he was representing someone else, who he would call Mr X for now, a person who was interested in contracting with me to undertake an assignment. Someone by the name of Serge Dubois was causing Mr X a lot of grief and he wanted me to scare him off somehow. He told me that Mr Dubois lived in Simiane la Rotunde, a tiny hamlet up north. I knew the location having visited it some years earlier."

"Carry on," Louis inserted.

"I told this Mr Camus that I might be interested. We discussed several scenarios. Camus told me that the intimidation technique had to be subtle because there could be no linkage back to Camus' boss. So, for example I couldn't beat up Serge and say something like – stop messing with Mr X. or get out of his way or the next time you won't be so lucky. There could be no way for Serge to connect the attack on him back to Mr X."

"That constraint limits the available options, I would have thought," Louis observed.

"Oui, exactement. Before we began to talk about various scenarios I wanted to know if this was worth my time and effort, so I asked Camus what was in this for me. He said no problem. The fee would be 130,000 French francs payable 65,000 francs up-front and 65,000 on completion. As you know, we are in the process of converting to the Euro so that would be roughly equivalent to €20,000 in total with €10,000 up-front, and €10,000 on completion – all in French francs cash. I thought that was reasonable and I knew that this would set me up perfectly to start to get my life back in order. I told him that we could negotiate around those numbers but that it was a good place to start. One always has to bargain, non?"

"Ha. Of course. What then?" Louis asked.

"We discussed a number of alternatives. I could meet him in a back alley somewhere and beat him up. The problem with that is he might chalk that up to a typical mugging or vandalism event. We kicked around a few other ideas. I could light a fire to his home but on closer examination I realized that in Simiane la Rotunde the houses and apartments in the centre of the town were all very close together – in typical middle ages style. A fire could spread and create a lot of unintended collateral damage. Serge could also get trapped and die in the fire. So, after kicking around a few other alternatives, we settled in on the plan for me to drive up to the Sault/Simiane la Rotunde area pour faire une reconnaissance and get an appreciation of Serge's typical movements. This could take a week and Camus undertook to reimburse me for all reasonable expenses. The scenario that we settled on, if it was feasible, was to run Serge off the road or highway somewhere, in an obvious move that would cause Dubois to think that the act was deliberate. From that he would hopefully conclude that Mr X was behind it. That was their goal – to spook and intimidate Serge and cause him to think that he should get out of Mr X's way and not bother him anymore," Maurice said.

"So, what happened next?" Louis queried.

"In the underground world there are no written contracts. A shake of the hands does it and God help someone if they renege. I decided that the 130,000 francs was a good deal. I told him the contract amount was acceptable but that once the job was complete, he would have to tell me who his boss was. I needed to know this to protect myself in the event that something unexpected happened and the project got de-railed or worse. Mr X would know who I was, and I needed to know his identity. He paused, and then reluctantly agreed. We shook hands. Camus came back the next day with 65,000 French francs in cash. I deposited 50,000 and kept the rest in my wallet. I then drove up to Sault and checked into a clean but cheap pension. I drove to

Simiane la Rotunde for the first few days, parked away from Serge's home, and kept a look-out for him and his movements. I noticed that he often drove to Sault to pick up groceries. There was not much shopping to be done in Simiane la Rotunde, so he went almost daily to Sault to the boucher et boulanger to pick up fresh bread and meat. I decided that I could position myself on the highway between Sault and Simiane la Rotunde in such a way that I could veer into his car on his way back from Sault."

"Did you find the spot you were looking for?" Louis asked.

"Yes, there was a point on Highway D-30 that looked to me to be ideal. It was a point in the road where it veered off to the left slightly. One kilometer before that curve, was a turn off area where I could park my car and wait for him to come by that part of the road. I could then take off behind him and force him off the road at that curve point. In the end that part worked out exactly as planned. I followed him to that corner and just before I pulled alongside of him as I passed, I looked at him and he looked at me and then I bumped my car against his and scraped the side of his car, I noticed his expression briefly and he was dumbfounded. I needed to act quickly to force him off the road so I then slammed the front end of my car sharply into his and he careened off the road. In that process my right fender got caught up in his bumper and it tore off the fender assembly completely. I was able to continue to drive, however, which I did for a kilometer or so. I drove back to the crash area and could see his car settled down in the small ravine off the main road somewhat. I decided not to head down there to have a look and to get out of there as fast as I could, so I took off. As I told you before I found a side road nearby, parked, slept through the night, and then headed off to Aix the next morning. And the rest is history as they say."

"Did Camus then complete his part of the deal?" Louis enquired.

"Yes, he did. He came by my house a few days later with the balance of 65,000 French francs in cash, plus an additional amount of 10,000 francs to cover estimated expenses, including the body work. I told him that I was concerned about my fender assembly that ended up on the crash site – not that I was worried necessarily about losing it, but the fact that it could create a linkage back to me. He told me his boss would take care of it. That was it. We shook hands and he disappeared."

Bourke continued, "I am trusting you that since I have told you the complete story, you will help me with the police. Will you do that?"

"Yes, I will. The matter of intent, or lack thereof, will certainly help you; together with the fact that you are cooperating to portray the whole series of events – and who was involved – will certainly help; and I will put your case forward in the best possible light," Louis committed. "Camus had promised to give you the identity of his boss. Did he do that? Who is Mister X?"

"Yes, he did. It is Alain Pelletier."

Chapter 32

Honest Ed

Nathan thought it was time to check back in with the management of Fairmont Hotels and Resorts in downtown Toronto to see where they were at with their assessment of the health spa proposal for Northern Provence. He put a call into Fairmont's Vice-President of Business Development, Cameron Sutton.

"Good to hear from you Nathan. Yes, we have reached a critical point in our evaluation of this project. Would you be able to come to our office sometime this week to discuss the matter?" Cameron asked.

"Yes, absolutely. Give me a day and time and I can probably do it," Nathan replied.

"Would tomorrow, Thursday, at 11 a.m. work for you?"

"Yes, that will be fine. You are at Wellington and Simcoe, I believe."

"Yes, exactly. See you tomorrow."

The next day Nathan found himself in the beautifully appointed corporate offices of the hotel chain in downtown Toronto.

"Let me get you up-to-date, Nathan, regarding the health spa project in Northern Provence. We have completed the first phase of our feasibility and business case analysis and the results are very encouraging. We believe that Northern Provence, with its rural setting and beautiful lavender fields, is the ideal location for upscale health spas. Our team has made successful presentations to our full management team, to our Board of Directors, and to the corporate people at the head office of our holding company. They have all been impressed and encouraging. We have the green light to proceed to the next steps. We would market the experience through our world-wide sales and marketing network. We believe also that such spas will rate well in Canada, and in particular in the largely French-speaking Province of Quebec," Cameron noted.

"That is excellent. What are the next steps, and are there ways in which my colleagues and I can assist?"

Cameron went into some detail describing the corporate culture of the Fairmont group, and the steps they take before making sizeable investments. He concluded by telling Nathan that the next step was to develop a bankable investment grade feasibility study. Since the company was not presently sitting on a lot of cash, and business conditions were not currently strong, they would need to bring in venture capital or at the least raise some mezzanine debt to finance this level of investment. Cameron advised that the next phase would involve another trip to Provence in the next two weeks so that the team could examine detailed logistics; they could purchase options on the sites they were interested in; meet with architects, engineers, quantity surveyors, and construction companies, to work up the detailed cost estimates and fine-tune the revenue forecasts, and do a number of other things.

"It would be great if you could accompany us Nathan, at least for the first part of our trip, perhaps assisted by your colleague in Avignon if that works, to make any important introductions and help us out with the local culture, geography, and logistics," Cameron proposed.

"I would be delighted to do this. I will check with Pierre, my friend in Avignon, and let you know by tomorrow," Nathan answered.

Nathan was elated. It looked like this project was proceeding. He thought of Serge and hoped he was looking down from Heaven, taking this all in. He would be thrilled. Nathan was sure of that.

Seeing that it was lunchtime, Nathan headed to a favourite restaurant of his in an area on Wellington Street to grab a bite. He was seated at a table next to another gentleman – sitting on his own as well. As Nathan looked over, he realized that the other loner was none other than his friend, and former university chum, Ed. The two of them had played football together, were members in the same fraternity, and had spent a lot of time together in the 1960's – especially since they both studied business and economics. The two of them had not stayed in close touch after university, but their paths had crossed a few times after graduation. Ed worked as a senior bond trader with a large Canadian investment banker – CIBC/Wood Gundy. He was the one with a seemingly self-destructive personality who had placed Nathan and his other pals into trouble on a number of occasions – one of the worst being when Nathan, Mort, Pierre, and Ed were called into the University Principal's office to be disciplined, and Ed almost blew it for all of them. In any case, the chemistry was good between them, there were some good memories, and Ed was a friend.

"Hi stranger," Nathan called over, "why don't you join me?"

"My God, fancy meeting you here. Great to see you. If I move over to join you does that mean that you are buying? Just kidding of course," Ed smiled as he joined Nathan at his table.

They spent the first fifteen minutes catching up on what they were currently up to, their families, and which fellow alumni they seen lately and what they were doing.

"Do you remember the time we were called into the Principal's office for a dressing down, and I pinched your rear end hard when you began to smile?" Nathan asked.

"Yes, I do. That was dicey, but we were young then – in our late teens. We have grown up since then," Ed said maturely.

"How about the time we ended up at this out-of-the-way bar miles from the university in a very rural part of the Eastern Townships. It was when we got into a big brawl," Nathan recollected.

"Funny, I don't remember that," Ed said.

Nathan remembered that evening vividly and he quickly replayed it in his mind while he sat there.

They were a group of six – all males and members of the same fraternity house and football team. They headed out one cold winter evening after wolfing down dinner in the university dining room. They took two cars and headed out of town. They traveled some distance until they came upon a bar in the middle of nowhere. In they went and sat at a large table. The place was packed and everyone there seemed to know each other – maybe an athletic team or social club they speculated. They were all Francophone, the exception being the six of them. After a few beers, Ed decided that he should dance.

He walked over to a table where two couples were sitting and asked a very attractive woman to dance. Her partner nodded and onto the dance floor they went. That was just the beginning. Right in front of the woman's boy friend, Ed reached around and grabbed his dancing partner by the rear end while they danced. We saw this happening and wondered what Ed was up to. Sure enough, the expression on the face of the boyfriend, the others at their table, and many others in the bar said it all. Suddenly they began talking amongst themselves and then about thirty young men stood up and shouted at Ed. Ed completely ignored them, he lost his dance partner, and very quickly a large group of angry young men were advancing on Ed and the group at their table.

The group knew they were badly outnumbered, so they formed a laager and headed towards the exit. Ed's view in situations like this was that one needed to be aggressive and when push came to shove, so to speak, it was important to get in the first punch. He lashed out at the closest opponent and pandemonium ensued. Nathan had travelled in Ed's car, so in between punches and some wrestling, the two of them managed to exit the bar and squeeze into the front seats. They were barely able to close the car doors, but finally Ed backed the car out quickly, avoiding the large swarming group. The bar parking lot was packed with cars, ploughed but still covered in light snow, and slippery. Ed had managed to get to the lot exit when he did a complete U turn, and with a laugh told Nathan that he was going to put the fear of God in the attackers. Nathan had just about fallen off his seat! Was Ed mad?!

Ed had driven back towards the chasing group, carefully avoiding them but causing them to jump out of the way. Close to the bar entrance, he did another quick U turn and they headed out to the lot exit for the second time with wheels spinning wildly. Nathan had turned to see what would then transpire, and sure enough, the angry mob was scrambling to get into their cars and follow them. He and Ed careened down the two-lane highway at great speed slipping and sliding along the way. Ed realized that he could not out-race the group of cars that was to follow so he took a fateful decision to make a quick left turn onto another narrow highway – and he did this before the chasing cars were in his rear-view mirror.

He and Ed had barrelled down this highway before Ed lost control and they careened hard into a ditch.

Nathan remembered that night vividly. With the car engine off, and both of them trying to push the car out of the ditch, the sky above was filled with sparkling stars.

The night was totally silent. They could almost hear the stars glistening. He and Ed stood there, realizing that getting the car back onto the highway would require some pushing and shoving time, while they watched with great glee as a group of six speeding cars went past the turn Ed had made and kept moving fast along the highway they had turned off. Ed and Nathan could hear the engines fade into the night thinking that at some point they would realize their mistake and turn back. It never happened. Nathan thought that it must have been an act of God, because otherwise, as he had said to Ed, they were dead men. The men from that bar were extremely angry and bent on revenge of that they were sure.

Finally, one half hour later, with much effort, they managed to get the car back on the road and return to the university.

On the way, Nathan had turned to Ed and said, "Are you mad? What were you thinking of? We got out of that one with the skin of our teeth."

Ed had turned to Nathan and laughed.

Coming back to the moment, Nathan was amazed that Ed could not recall this event as it was etched in Nathan's psyche. Maybe it was just denial.

Nathan and Ed told a few more funny stories and then took their leave. They still enjoyed each others' company.

Chapter 33

Into focus

The weekly Skype conference call was set for Friday at 2 p.m. Jacques welcomed everyone once all were on-line.

"Bonne après-midi, Pierre et Jacques, et bonjours Nathan."

Pierre, Nathan, and Louis reciprocated the salutation and Jacques asked Louis to begin the briefing.

Louis began, "Much has happened since our last conference call. I have had two more meetings with Maurice Bourke and he has been most helpful. In fact, I wonder if he has gone soft in the head while in prison, he has been so cooperative. Alternatively, he has a form of death wish that causes him to want to return to prison – he has spent half of his life there already. The other explanation is that he knows that he is hemmed-in and wants to leverage his ability to cooperate to his advantage."

Jacques interrupted from Paris, "Don't be immodest, Louis. I am sure that your skills and experience are playing a big part in moving this forward."

"It's kind of you to say that. I am sure that doesn't hurt."

Louis then related to the group the substance of the meetings and discussions he had had with Maurice Bourke on the two recent occasions.

"Do you think Bourke is now telling the truth?" Pierre asked.

"I think so. It is not entirely clear to me, however, whether they just wanted to scare Serge, or whether they wanted him dead. That may become more obvious as we proceed further," Louis replied.

"Did you discover who Mr X is?" Jacques asked.

"Yes, I did, but before that Bourke pleaded with me, and made me commit to put his best foot forward to the police when it became an active police investigation. I told him I would, and that the question of intent, or lack thereof, would work in his favour – if it was true – together with the fact that he was cooperating by describing the whole series of events, and who was involved. I undertook to put his case forward in the best possible light. With those assurances he told me that his boss, Mr X, was Alain Pelletier," Louis replied.

"My God. Pelletier is the President of HELIVOL!" exclaimed Jacques.

"You are right. Absolutely. How enlightening!" Nathan added.

"If Pelletier is behind this, it means that he and HELIVOL were very upset with Serge's protest group and they wanted to either intimidate him or get rid of him. Is that not a reasonable conclusion to come to?" Pierre asked.

“D’accord. Agreed,” they all chimed in.

As this discussion was taking place, Nathan was tapping on his laptop in Toronto and googling HELIVOL.

“Holy cow,” Nathan exclaimed, “I know this guy, Pelletier, and I’ve just connected the dots. A moment ago I went onto HELIVOL’s web site and found Pelletier’s photograph as CEO. This is someone who I went to school with and who was my least favourite person. In France he has tweaked his first name to Alain. In Montreal he was known as Allan Pelletier. He was, and obviously still is, an unsavoury character,” Nathan asserted.

“What an extraordinary coincidence. Maybe we can use this to advantage,” Jacques observed.

“I believe we can,” Nathan confirmed.

Louis entered back into the conversation, “Before we get too far ahead of ourselves, I need to point out that we are precipitously close to having to report all of this to the Police Nationale,” he cautioned.

“I understand, but I have an idea,” Nathan said.

Chapter 34

Don Quixote

Nathan was shocked to learn that his former nemesis was intimately involved in the tragedy that occurred in Northern Provence, resulting in the death of his friend, Serge. The group on the Skype call the day before had decided to let the information from Louis sink in and had set up a conference call for the next day. Nathan decided to join the call from his downtown office because he had arranged a meeting with his partner, Mike, to follow the Skype call. He was out of bed at 6, showered and shaved, had a light breakfast, and was walking to the Toronto subway station closest to his home, just a few blocks away. It was a glorious early August morning with not a cloud in the sky and the temperature already hovering at twenty degrees Celsius.

Sitting on the subway on the way to his office Nathan thought about the latest development and was not surprised that Allan Pelletier would do something like this.

In his downtown office, he signed into the Skype call. When the four of them, Jacques, Pierre, Louis, and Nathan were all connected, Jacques welcomed everyone and called the meeting to order.

Nathan interjected, "Before we start into the main business, I should give all of you an update on the status of Fairmont Hotels and Resorts evaluation of an investment in health spas in Northern Provence. This may not be of great interest to Louis, so I will keep it short and to the point, and send a more detailed summary to you, Jacques, and Pierre, later today. Is that OK?"

"Yes, proceed," Jacques approved.

"Last week I decided that it was time to check in with Fairmont so I called their VP Business Development, Cameron Sutton, and he told me progress was very positive and he asked me if I could come down to their office, which I did. The bottom line is that Fairmont wants to move forward with this. They have made successful presentations to their Board and holding company and been given the green light to go to the next step. Management needs to complete what they refer to as a bankable investment grade feasibility study. Cameron and a small Fairmont team will soon travel to Northern Provence again and spend a couple of weeks there. During that time, they will negotiate purchase options on the sites they are interested in; and meet with architects, engineers, quantity surveyors, and construction companies, to work-up the detailed cost estimates and fine-tune the revenue forecasts. They have asked Pierre and me to join them on the first part of the visit to make any needed introductions, and assist them with the local culture, geography, and so on. I have agreed to do this and have tentatively booked flights for next week. Does all of that make sense to all of you? Will you be available, Pierre, next week to participate as Fairmont has requested?" Nathan queried.

"This sounds very positive," Jacques noted.

"I am happy to participate in the tour as needed, and when you are here, Nathan, you can make our home in Avignon your base camp if you like. Suzanne and I would he happy to host you. Normally we leave Avignon at the end of June, but we have decided this year to stay until mid-September. I need more time to complete the gazebo and garden shed that I am building on the back of my property. Besides, we could use the opportunity to get caught up with you at the same time," offered Pierre.

"Pierre, that is truly kind of you. Consider it a done deal. I should say to you Jacques, that you are most welcome to join our little group if you are interested and available," Nathan said, not sure if Pierre wasn't just being a very good friend by staying on, and feeling somewhat guilty.

"Merci, Nathan, but I will pass at this time. I think the two of you will represent us very well," Jacques offered.

"Great. Pierre and I will coordinate on logistics and make this happen. Now, Gentlemen, I do not wish to dominate the conversation, but you will recall that after the briefing by Louis yesterday, I mentioned that I had an idea. Would it be OK if I described that now? I can do it at the end of the meeting if that is preferred, but what

I propose might impact our discussion overall," Nathan mentioned.

"As far as I'm concerned, I would like to have your thoughts on this now. Pierre and Louis, are you OK to proceed this way?" Jacques asked.

Pierre and Louis indicated their agreement.

"Well, as I told you yesterday, I know this Alain quite well. We went to school together in Montreal and played hockey on the same team. As you gathered, he is not my favourite person, to put it mildly. Now I know that Louis, you would like to file a report with the Police Nationale in Aix sooner rather than later. I understand that. But here is what I propose. When in Northern Provence next week I will contact Alain through his HELIVOL office in Aix and through his secretary or executive assistant, tell them that I am an old friend from Canada visiting Northern Provence, and see if I can arrange a time when I can take him out to dinner in Aix. He may or may not agree, but I'm not sure that he is completely aware of my lingering animosity towards him. I will be very nice. My thinking is that over a few glasses of wine with dinner, he might let his guard down and tell me more than he should. I will wait until he is slurring his words somewhat before I ask him if he had heard about the horrible car accident near Sault in May. From there I will have to play it by ear as they say. For this dinner, I would like to get wired up with a listening device and record our conversation. I am sure that Louis can help me with this. As you can probably guess, Alain is a bit of a braggard, so he might have loose lips. It is worth a try, I believe, and it will only add one more week before Louis goes to the police. With any luck he can go to them with a rock-solid case against Pelletier as well. One of the missing pieces for me is whether the plan was to spook Serge, or to eliminate him. Certainly, Pelletier knows the answer to that. How does that sound?"

"I think it is worth a try. It could be very fruitful. I agree with you, Nathan, that Pelletier could have contracted with Bourke to get rid of Serge completely. I, for one, definitely want an answer to that one. Bourke might well be lying about this to save his skin," Jacques commented.

"I'm in," asserted Pierre.

"Fine with me as long as this doesn't drag on too much longer. I can come up with a listening device. Not to get too far ahead, but what would you plan to wear to such a dinner? Clothing dictates how we would wire you up," Louis asked.

"Typically, I would wear an open shirt and summer weight sports jacket and slacks. Will that work?"

"Yes, fine. I will start working on that. I have some of that equipment myself and otherwise I can get it."

As they signed off, Nathan committed to keeping the group informed. He was pleased with the result and wandered down to partner Mike's office for his next meeting.

"Come on in," Mike invited.

"Thanks."

"How is your project in Provence coming together?" Mike enquired.

"We are making excellent progress on all fronts. Thanks for asking."

Nathan continued, "I wanted to leave you with a draft report to the World Bank that I have been working on. You may recall about eighteen months ago, our firm was hired by them to do some governance work in Russia. You were tied up at the time, so I took it on, and Claire, our Associate, joined me on the project. Do you recall that?"

"Yes, I do, but I lost track of the project after that, given my workload at that time."

"Yes, well the Speakers of both the Russian State Duma and the Russian Federation Council, approached the World Bank about two years ago and asked them for some help in increasing the capacity and skill sets of Russia's Accounts Chamber. Now, the Accounts Chamber in Russia is equivalent to Canada's Auditor-General, or what is referred to in the USA as the Government Accountability Office, or GAO. These institutions are charged with enhancing accountability by conducting independent audits of government operations. They typically report to the nation's Parliament or Congress, not the Executive Branch. The two Russian Speakers were concerned that their Accounts Chamber needed some help to improve their performance. The fact that the Russian Government had large amounts of debt owing to the World Bank influenced the Bank to approve the project. Our firm bid on the job and we were successful."

"Good stuff. I am curious about the project – what it comprised of and how it went."

"The head of the Accounts Chamber, and his staff, were very cooperative when we arrived in Moscow.

They were keen and recognized that they had work to do to get to a level of competence and performance equivalent to comparable institutions in other countries. As we conversed with them, it became clear that their work was focused on checking whether or not invoices or vouchers were approved by the right authority and whether or not they had been signed off correctly, and things of that nature. In contrast, as you know, Canada's Auditor-General perform those functions also, but, in addition, they perform high-level management audits and comprehensive audits, and often value-for-money audits."

"I can see a huge gap in the capacity of the Accounts Chamber when compared with our Auditor-General. Obviously, they had not done any audits of Russian privatizations."

"Interesting that you should bring up that topic. At different meetings with the leader of the Accounts Chamber and his staff, I asked if they had ever done an audit of a privatization. I never once got a straight answer, even though these people were very committed to improving their performance. I concluded that even though they were willing to take on challenges to enhance the government's transparency and accountability, privatizations were, for the moment, off limits. Of course, one can understand the sensitivity around privatizations in Russia. In fact, most of the large privatizations had already been executed under Boris Yeltsin's watch – to former members of the KGB and other oligarchs. It is also generally acknowledged that most or all of the privatizations were *bent* – that is, sold at non-arms length at significantly undervalued prices. The attitude of the Accounts Chamber was, however, that while the leader and his staff were keen to grow, it would have to be one step at a time," Nathan said.

"Makes sense."

"The end result of all of this was our recommendation that an exchange program be established between Russia's Accounts Chamber and Canada's Auditor-General. The goal was for the Accounts Chamber to observe how the Auditor-General operated, learn from that, and build their skill sets and approaches to audit. Both Speakers of the Russian Parliament endorsed this idea, as did the World Bank; introductions were made and the interchange began. The program operated, back and forth, staff from both countries moving between Russia and Canada, very successfully for about one and a half years. This success story ended last week, however, when we were told that President Vladimir Putin had decided that the Accounts Chamber from now on would report to him, and not to the State Duma and Federation Council. This basically negated all the good work that had been accomplished to date. Very disappointing."

"I can understand how that decision would be a bombshell. Afterall, the whole idea of an Accounts Chamber, or Auditor-General is for it to be independent of the Executive Branch of the Government. The Government is the body being audited on behalf of the people, as represented by Parliament or Congress, so it cannot have a say in what is to be audited or reported."

"You've got it. In any case I have written-up what is, unfortunately, the final report to the World Bank on the project, and I wondered if you could have a look at it sometime. No great rush – just when you are able."

"Not a problem. I am happy to do this. Any other stories or enjoyable experiences to describe when you were in Russia?"

"I have one funny story and a couple of experiences to relate. The Accounts Chamber amazingly has a very modest museum outside their reception area in Moscow. I wandered around and discovered that this institution has been around in Russia since the time of the Tsars. I was curious, given the authority and coersive powers of the Tsars, how they would react to negative audit reports. In response to this question, I was told that in that era the Accounts Chamber was focused exclusively in accounting for the inventories in the granaries!" Nathan laughed.

"That is much more plausible!"

"My wife, Erika, accompanied me on this trip. When I was in meetings during the day, she did some sightseeing and traveled around Moscow often on the subway or, Moscow Metro. The metro stations are fabulously decorated with tiled frescoes, marble columns and ornate chandeliers. Together we enjoyed two great experiences. The State Duma hosted us, together with our colleague, Claire, to a performance of the ballet Don Quixote at the Bolshoi Ballet. That was the experience of a lifetime. We almost had to pinch ourselves, just being at the Bolshoi Theatre in Moscow. Also, when my work in Moscow was completed, Erika and I took the midnight train from Moscow to Saint Petersburg. We spent three days there and we went all out by hiring a guide and a driver to show us around. That is a beautiful and amazing city. I must say Russia, with all of its faults and challenges, is rich in culture and history."

"Well at least you have some good memories to compensate. Had you been to Russia before?"

"Yes, a few times previously, but those visits have not generated many very fond memories, apart from just experiencing the vastness and cultural richness of Russia. Before we formed our partnership, I was engaged as a consultant from 1991 to 1992 to work with a forest products company, Miranda Forest, whose business strategy was to take advantage of then President Mikhail Gorbachev's glasnost and perestroika reform policies that were designed to open and liberalize the economy. The idea was that with a more open society, the demand for paper and packaging products would increase significantly. The company had a strategic partner in Montreal that manufactured pulp mill refiners, so the partners settled on a project to build a pulp mill in Russia. I believe the strategy was sound; it was just that doing business at that time in Russia was exceedingly difficult. In fact, while we were there developing a feasibility study, the U.S.S.R. disintegrated. By way of example of the instability, one day we were dealing with the Soviet Union's state development corporation – The Vnesheconombank – and the next day it was a Russian institution! Government controlled prices were being eliminated but no one would hazard a guess where wholesale prices were headed. In that environment how does one estimate the costs of chemicals, power, and other inputs? My client's Russian partner at that time had no hard currency cash so any so-called in-kind contributions by the Russian state were consistently over-valued. The rouble was considered worthless, so the demand for hard currency throughout the supply chain was impossible to responsibly meet. The Russians had little comprehension of how a market economy works. I recall a morning meeting when we worked for three hours on defining for the Russians what the term working capital meant. Government representatives also brought up the possibility of a Super Profits Tax which bore no resemblance to concepts of risk/reward. I could go on and on, but won't."

"It sounds almost impossible," Mike commented.

"Yes, it was, and my client pulled out based on my recommendation before making any serious investments. Anecdotally, the Russia/USA or Canadian dollar/Russian rouble official exchange rates were very seldom used, whereas the black-market rate was king. I recall, however, one evening in Moscow when our team decided to enjoy a pizza at the Pizza Hut in the centre of town. Pizza Hut had both a hard currency and a rouble pizza parlour, side-by-side served by the same kitchen. A line-up formed to get into the rouble hut, so we opted for the hard currency side – no line up there! There were five of us. We ordered two large pizzas, two beers each, apple pie with ice cream and coffee all around. When I came to settle the bill, it amounted to about US$150. I told the check-out counter clerk that there must be some mistake. Not so, I learned, because the rouble menu was translated for the purposes of the bill into US dollars using the fictitious official exchange rate. I couldn't make a fuss since we were negotiating with the Russian Government on the business deal, and I didn't want to create an issue that could go public. Interestingly, once or twice we bumped into the Canadian George Cohon in Moscow. He was setting up the McDonald's business there and he wisely opted for a rouble business only. That is why there were huge line-ups when he launched the first McDonald's restaurant in Moscow. We assumed that he was counting on the periodic currency auctions that the Russian Government organized as a way to repatriate some cash back to Canada. But in the meantime, the corporate strategy was to backward integrate into the complete supply chain. This was a way to control quality and to buy some time until there was an easing of currency controls, and when the rouble had more value, hopefully sometime in the future. Anyway, lots of stories, but I have taken up enough of your time. Thanks for reading over my World Bank report. Give me a call when you are ready," Nathan concluded.

"Sure enough. Will do. Great speaking with you as usual. Have a great rest of the day."

They parted.

Chapter 35

TGV

Nathan checked into his Air Canada flight to Paris at Pearson International Airport in Toronto. From Paris to Avignon he had booked le Train à Trés Grande Vitesse (TGV), operated by the French Government's Société nationale des chemins de fer français (SNCF), from Aéroport Charles de Gaulle to Avignon. The connections at Charles de Gaulle airport to the TGV, and to almost all modes of transportation, were excellent and easy. The train trip was typically between two and one half and three hours, depending on the train and the stops, which, when compared to air travel to the same destination, was very competitive. He preferred to travel by rail whenever he could. Pierre and Suzanne had offered to collect him at the TGV train station in Avignon. He had declined their kind offer and had opted to rent a car to drive to their home.

"Bienvenue, Nathan, dans notre maison," Pierre and Suzanne offered their welcome, followed by big hugs.

They retired to the back patio into comfortable chairs, each with a glass of great Grenache Noir wine.

"So, how was the trip?" Pierre asked.

"Uneventful, which is the preferred way to travel. How are both of you?" Nathan replied, and asked.

"We are doing well," Suzanne replied. "We very much enjoy living in this area for part of the year, and the gardening which I enjoy keeps me busy. We often have visitors here, like yourself, who we enjoy immensely. We had an enjoyable time with houseguests, friends of ours from Montreal who were here in April."

"Glad to hear you had a good trip getting here. I have been enjoying the fly fishing in and around Avignon, the touring about, and I do help Suzanne out in the garden."

"I see that the gazebo and garden shed that you are building are both progressing well. They should be really useful and attractive additions to your back yard."

"Thanks. Yes, they are coming along. This is a project that has been begging to be completed, but the fishing, and touring around, have been getting in the way."

Pierre continued, "Well, we certainly have some interesting developments in the circumstances surrounding Serge's death, and Louis' investigation."

"Isn't that the truth! I think Louis has been doing a great job and his experience is showing. It was also his hard work, and thoroughness, that landed him at *Auto Plus*, and his friend Arthur. He then followed-up diligently and used his considerable skills to get the suspect to talk. I am also looking forward to meeting up with Alain Pelletier in the next few days. Not that I am a vindictive person, but maybe I can settle a few scores. More importantly, for me and I'm sure for all of us, it is critical to nail down whether the charges that the police will lay down will be for murder or manslaughter. With any luck, he will let his guard down and answer this important question – was the plan to kill Serge, or to cause him serious injury? Either is bad, but murder obviously the worst case. Hopefully he will agree to my invitation to dinner."

"What are the chances?" Pierre asked.

"I would say 50/50 or better. We will know soon. The first thing to do is for me to call Louis tomorrow and find out if he has a listening device organized for me, and if not, how much time he needs. Presumably I can use your land line to make some calls. Would that be OK?"

"Of course," Suzanne and Pierre answered in unison.

"Tomorrow I will call Cameron Sutton, the Fairmont VP, on his cell phone and see what, if anything, he has in mind for you and me, Pierre, over the next few days. I suspect that there won't be a lot, but he wanted us to be available in case a particular circumstance presented itself to him and his team, and he needed our advice or help. Those two calls – to Louis and Cameron – will determine when I call Pelletier and seek a dinner date with him. If he agrees to dinner, I will book a hotel room in Aix for that night, so I can feel free to drink a lot of wine with Alain with no pressure thinking about the drive back to Avignon."

"We can recommend a couple of hotels for you. It sounds like a good plan to stay overnight. Now, if you will excuse me, I am heading to the kitchen to prepare dinner. The two of you can carry on with your conversation. We will probably eat out here on the patio, and for that I will call you, Pierre, to give me a hand bringing out the food. Excusez-moi," Suzanne said.

"I can help too," Nathan offered.

Pierre and Nathan topped up their wine glasses and switched topics.

"Pierre, traveling to Avignon on the TGV reminded me of the brief discussions we had when you were on the Board of VIA Rail Canada. Were you not looking at a TGV to run in the corridor? I believe the corridor is defined as Quebec City to Montreal to Ottawa to Toronto and then finally to Windsor. Is that so?" Nathan asked.

"Yes, that's correct, with the leg to Windsor considered a later add-on. As you know I stepped down from the VIA Board a couple of years ago, but I still stay in touch with the folks there."

Pierre continued, "Interestingly, I am told that the French Government's Société nationale des chemins de fer français TGV route from Paris to Marseilles, which is just around the corner from here, and one of the more popular TGV routes in France, is the only one in the whole of France that makes money for SNCF. The French Government pours billions of francs into the SNCF passenger rail operations each year and it reports huge annual losses. But getting back to VIA, the problem that VIA had, and still has, is the congestion in the corridor. Most of the trackage in the corridor is owned by CN Rail. VIA pays CN a fee to use their tracks. The problem is that the corridor tracks are heavily used by freight trains, and the number of slots available to VIA is limited. This is compounded by the fact that passenger trains require 3-4 times the capacity of freight trains because they travel at higher speeds, and more space is needed between trains. The problem is exacerbated by the fact that in Canada freight trains take priority over passenger trains, meaning that when there is competition for trackage, CN and CP get the nod, which often results in VIA trains pulling into sidings while freight trains pass. This plays havoc with VIA's schedules, and it's on-time performance commitments. CN has been reluctant to provide VIA with more slots, or departure times and gates, at Union Station in Toronto, and Central Station in Montreal, for example. For this and other reasons, a Canadian consortium consisting of Bombardier, together with the engineering consulting company SNC Lavalin, and others, developed a proposal to build a TGV, on completely new tracks, through the corridor. Their concept was very creative but it had a big price tag – upwards of $11 billion. The plan was to run French-technology TGV trains at 320 kilometers an hour. The engineers had all the rail crossings going over or under roads, with only one level crossing – a positive feature since level crossings and TGV's do not mix well. If I recall correctly, under their scenario, the time to travel from Montreal to Toronto was just over two hours, and that was of course downtown to downtown. Their proposed tiered price points were also very competitive."

"Sounds like a great idea. What happened to the consortium's proposal?" Nathan queried.

"It all came down to dollars, as these things often do. To make this happen and to finance the project, the proponents would have needed financial guarantees of $8 billion, not cash, from the Canadian federal government. This was just too rich for the leaders in Ottawa. Dropping this project was really unfortunate and will come back to haunt us as a country at a later date, I believe. VIA Rail is the independent Crown corporation that is legally mandated to operate intercity passenger rail service in Canada, so there were obviously conversations taking place at this time between the Bombardier/Lavalin consortium and VIA."

"So where does VIA sit with all of this now. It sounds like the problem would not have gone away," commented Nathan.

"Exactly. There is now a move afoot to build a less than TGV speed train set of dedicated tracks in the corridor – dedicated to VIA. I think this is ultimately what it will come down to. The challenge will be for VIA to finance this, and the costs understandably are increasing. It could be possible, however, with some significant federal/provincial infrastructure money. Clearly, Ontario and Quebec, in addition to Canada as a whole, will benefit from this transportation option."

At this point, a call came from the kitchen.

"Pouvez-vous m'aider?" called Suzanne.

Off they went to carry trays and continue the discussion at another time.

Chapter 36

Relais & Châteaux

Recovering from a delicious but rather large dinner the night before, Suzanne had suggested some fruit and yoghurt for breakfast the next morning. Nathan heartily agreed. They sat around the kitchen table, enjoying the light breakfast, and talked.

"Thank you for a wonderful evening yesterday and a great dinner. Much appreciated," Nathan commented.

"Our pleasure," Suzanne answered.

"Suzanne, you were born and raised in Grenoble, so I was wondering if you and Pierre get to travel there often? Do you still have relatives there?"

"Thanks for asking", Suzanne replied. "My father died several years ago, but my mother is quite healthy and still living in Grenoble where she stays in a seniors' residence. One of my sisters, and one brother, left Grenoble a while back, but one married sister is still there, and she sees, and attends to my mother very capably. My brother lives in Paris, and my other sister lives in Montreal, not far from us. When Pierre and I are here in Avignon we do get to see my mother, and my sister. It is just over a two-hour drive to Grenoble, so when we go there we usually stay with my sister. Also, ma mère comes and stays with us here in our home in Avignon for a week each year. It's not perfect, but it works out very well, all things considered."

"Wonderful. Families are often spread out so far apart these days. I have similar challenges with my spread-out family."

"Nathan, Suzanne and I are planning, after breakfast, to go on what one might call either a long walk or a short hike in the Avignon area. We will be back before lunch. Are you able to join us? I know you need to make some phone calls today."

"I would love to. It is such a beautiful day, and I would like to see more of the Avignon area. I don't have any hiking gear, but I have a pair of good walking shoes with me and a hat. Will that suffice?" Nathan asked.

"Great. What we have in mind is to start at the Avignon City train station ending up at the beautiful Place du Palais. Along the way we will pass by the Fondation Calvet, the Rue de la Peyrolerie, the Chapelle des Pénitents noirs, the Pont D'Avignon, the Rocher des Domes, the Hotel des Monnaies, and the Place du Palais. That return trip would be about five miles, but we can cut it short if need be. Does that sound reasonable? Do you do much walking in Toronto? I know there are great hiking trails through the Don River Valley and Humber River Valley systems," Pierre commented.

"I am definitely in. Yes, Erika and I do a lot of walking in Toronto and we really enjoy it. Helps to keep one fit as well."

After tidying up the kitchen after breakfast, they headed out in Pierre's car to travel to the train station, the starting point for their walk. Nathan thought the hike was fantastic. There was so much history and beauty to absorb, and such a gorgeous day to do it in. They arrived back at Pierre and Suzanne's home a few hours later, somewhat tired but elated. For lunch Erika prepared a selection of croque monsieur and croque madame sandwiches – essentially grilled ham and cheese topped with a white sauce. Nathan particularly liked the croque madame with the poached egg on top. A sexist thought passed through his mind – why wasn't the croque with the egg on top dubbed the croque monsieur instead of croque madame? Was an egg on top a guy thing? How dumb to even think that, and why?

After lunch, Nathan excused himself to make a few phone calls. Pierre offered him his den so he could work undisturbed. The first call was to Louis.

"Bonjours, Louis. Comment ça va?" Nathan asked.

"Très biens merci, et toi?"

"Great thanks. Louis, I will be calling Alain Pelletier soon to see if I can arrange a dinner with him. Have you located a *wire*, or concealed listening device for me?"

"I have, but it would fit much better if you wore a tie," Louis replied.

"OK. I get it. If I took Pelletier to a four- or five-star restaurant – a Relais & Châteaux par example – I would wear a tie. There must be such a thing in Aix, not so?" Nathan asked.

"Absolument, there is, and I can recommend the perfect spot – very elegant and quiet – *La Villa Gallici*. Pelletier would be very impressed with your choice, and they have some excellent wines, as you can imagine!"

"Great idea. Let's do it then. I will call back after I have spoken to Pelletier and arranged a date and time for our dinner. We could then book a time for me to get fitted with the device. I will make the dinner reservation. I am sure Pierre and Suzanne will have the coordinates for this establishment or I can get it off their web page. Thanks so much, Louis. À la prochaine."

The next call was to Cameron Sutton, the Fairmont VP, on his cell phone.

"Hello, Cameron. Are you settling in well? Where are you and your team at this moment?" Nathan enquired.

"Hi. Thanks for the call. We just arrived yesterday, and we are staying at a gîte just outside of Sault. It is very comfortable here and we can cook our own meals. There is also a desk and a large table here that will come in useful. Are you at your friend's home in Avignon?"

"Yes, I just arrived also and I am being taken incredibly good care of. I am calling to say hello but also to ask whether or not you will be needing Pierre or myself in the next few days."

"I don't think so. Next week might be another question. Right now we are just getting oriented and getting our feet on the ground so to speak."

"Perfect. I have a couple of things to do over the next few days, but you can always reach us at Pierre's home, or on our cells," Nathan said.

"Sure, that's fine. We will talk again in a couple of days. Be well," Cameron dialed out.

Now Nathan could put the call into Alain Pelletier. He dialed the main switchboard and asked for Monsieur Pelletier.

"Let me direct your call to his office," came the reply.

"Oui, bonjour. Puis-Je vous aider?"

"Yes, is it OK if we speak en Anglais?" Nathan asked.

"Of course. How can I help you?" came the response from what Nathan assumed was Pelletier's Secretary or Executive Assistant.

"My name is Nathan Callahan. This is a personal call. I am an old friend of Mr Pelletier from Montreal and I would like to say hello to him," Nathan said.

"Yes, one moment please. Can I put you on hold?"

A moment later Alain Pelletier was at the other end of the phone.

"Mon dieu, a voice from the past. How in the hell are you?" Pelletier blurted out.

"I am very well, and how are you?"

"Very busy, but in business that is usually a good thing," Pelletier said.

"I won't keep you then, but I am in Avignon visiting with friends here. I will be making a trip one afternoon to Aix, and I wondered if I could take you out for dinner that evening in Aix. There is much water under the bridge as they say, and I thought it would be a great opportunity to catch up. Are you free?" Nathan asked.

"Yes, a late dinner tomorrow evening in Aix would work. The day after that I'm traveling," Pelletier replied.

"Great! I will call your office later today or tomorrow morning and give your Assistant the time, and the restaurant coordinates if that is OK." Nathan was very happy.

"Perfect. I look forward to it. Bye."

Nathan hung up and rushed in to tell Pierre.

"We are having dinner tomorrow evening in Aix! One more step forward."

Chapter 37

Le diner

After speaking with Pelletier, Nathan made a dinner reservation for the next day at 8 p.m. at *La Villa Gallici* in Aix. He decided to bite a bullet and stay over at the same location as it operated as a hotel as well. It wouldn't be an inexpensive evening, but *c'est la vie.*

He then called Alain Pelletier's Executive Assistant and gave the dinner details to her. She told Nathan that she would pass along the message to Mr Pelletier, and that he had already told her to hold that evening open. He would be very pleased – *La Villa Gallici* was Mr Pelletier's favourite restaurant. He would meet Nathan at the restaurant at 8 p.m. She asked for Nathan's coordinates in case anything unusual came up, but she thought not.

Next, he called Louis. They agreed to meet at Louis' home at 3 pm the next day – just before Nathan checked into the hotel – at which time Nathan would be fitted with the *wire.*

Just so that everyone was up-to-date, Nathan sent an e-mail message to Jacques telling him about the pending dinner with Pelletier.

Jacques replied, "Bonne chance mon ami!"

For the remainder of the afternoon, Suzanne, Pierre and Nathan sat out on the back patio and enjoyed the beautiful afternoon. Pierre asked Nathan for his help holding a couple of boards while he lined them up and screwed them onto the frame of the gazebo he was building.

As they sat around, Nathan told Pierre and Suzanne that he had heard through the grapevine that the Government of Canada was drafting legislation, likely to be dubbed the *Clarity Act*, that would make more clear what the conditions and criteria would be before the federal government would enter into negotiations with a province, like Quebec, that might be desirous of leaving the Canadian federation. Nathan observed that this bill was in response to the separatist movement in Quebec, and the referendum that was held in the Province of Quebec in 1995 that came very close to a win for the YES side.

"As a former Montrealer, that was too close for comfort for me. As Montrealers currently you may feel the same. Do you think such legislation is a good idea?" Nathan queried.

Suzanne was first out of the blocks. "The separatist threat never seems to go away which is not totally surprising given that Francophones in the Province of Quebec comprise over 75% of the population. Some French-speaking persons are worried that their language and culture is threatened given that they are surrounded by a sea of Anglophones. To me, though, separation is not the answer."

"Yes, and don't forget the so-called Allophones – those whose mother tongue is neither English nor French – who now make up over 13% of Quebec's population. But I agree with Suzanne that separation by Quebec from the rest of Canada is the wrong approach. It seems to me also that this is the wrong time to bring in legislation like the *Clarity Act* that you have described. Since the 1995 referendum, there has been less talk of separation. Young people in Quebec are more focused on jobs and economic security and many of them believe they are better off in a united Canada. You know the old adage – *let sleeping dogs lie,"* Pierre contributed.

"It is interesting that you say that Pierre, because I am told on good authority that the federal government believes that this is the best time to act – when emotions are dormant and citizens are focused on other matters. Suzanne, I would like to pick up on what you said. If not separation, what?"

"The whole world is realizing that a large critical mass is needed to wield economic power. A good example is the formation of the European Union. Canada is a large country geographically – the second largest country in the world by area, after Russia I believe, but we have a relatively small population, at about 34 million. Having said that, we typically *play above our weight class* economically. We are the world's tenth largest economy and we are a member of the G-7, made up of the seventh largest advanced world economies. Why leave that advantage behind? Additionally, many of the younger people today recognize that in the world of information technology and computers, English is the dominant language. I think that many of the steps that the Quebec government has taken to date will help to preserve the French language and culture. While I find the language laws often juvenile, I think it is fair for new immigrants coming to Quebec to be required to speak French, or to learn to speak French. The Quebec Government also invests heavily in cultural and linguistic institutions in Quebec, and to me those are positive and essential steps," Suzanne answered.

"Good points," Pierre and Nathan volunteered.

"Now, it is quickly approaching happy hour. Instead of wine, which we will have for dinner, anyone for a pre-dinner cocktail? I would recommend Pierre's martinis. He is often complimented on them. Any takers?" Suzanne asked?

"Bingo! How about a dry gin martini for me?" Nathan asked.

"With a couple of olives?" Pierre asked.

"Absolument. Thanks."

The three of them sat around for some time, sipping on martinis, in advance of a great dinner of steak-frites on the back patio, and simultaneously solving all of the world's problems.

Chapter 38

The meeting

A relaxing morning reading the International Herald Tribune, and catching up on reading his book, was spent by Nathan. Suzanne puttered in the garden and Pierre worked on building his shed. They shared a light lunch of a sandwich and salad. Nathan then packed a small overnight bag, and a garment bag holding his sports jacket, shirt, tie and trousers. It was about a one-hour drive from Avignon to Aix so he left in his rental car at 1:45 pm so that he could drive casually and reach Louis' home by 3 pm.

The weather was perfect again, and the drive to Aix enjoyable. Nathan had loaded Louis' home address into the car's built-in GPS so he could relax at the wheel, follow the prompts, and enjoy the scenery. He reached Louis' home, a small cottage styled residence built on an attractive property with a low-maintenance garden with shrubs, just before 3 p.m. Louis greeted him and showed him into his living room. Nathan went into a guest bedroom and changed into his sports jacket attire for the fitting. The wire fit very compactly and invisibly behind his tie such that Nathan felt very confident that it would not be detected. Louis took him through the routine about turning it on and off, the volume setting, and so on, and told him the batteries were good for up to four hours.

Nathan changed back into his travel clothes and headed over to the hotel to check-in. Although *La Villa Gallici* restaurant's cuisine was French, and more specifically French Provence offerings, the property had an Italian feel to it. The hotel was set on a beautifully manicured verdant site with Roman carved statues strategically located. A valet driver relieved Nathan of his car, and a bellman of his bag, and Nathan headed to the reception area to sign in. He had opted for a small room – it was just for one night, but the appointments and set-up of his room were luxurious. They should be for the price he was paying he thought. He decided to lie on the bed, read his book, and maybe have a nap before dinner.

He headed to the restaurant a few minutes before 8 p.m. and, with the help of the Maître d'hôtel, chose a quiet candle-lit table on the terrace. Nathan told the Maître that he was expecting Alain and to direct him to this table when he arrived.

"Ah oui, Monsieur Pelletier. Je le connais bien. I know him well," he said. The setting was perfect and seemed the ideal time to order a pre-dinner cocktail – a martini was ordered.

A few minutes later, Alain was standing by Nathan's table. Earlier, Nathan had turned on the listening device and checked that it was not visible.

"Well, hello stranger, it has been a while," Pelletier said as the two of them shook hands.

"Yes, it sure has. Hi and thanks for doing this."

"My pleasure. Thanks for the invitation."

Alain ordered a double Lagavulin sixteen-year old single malt Scotch whiskey, neat.

"So, what brings you here to Provence?" Alain asked.

"My wife, Erika, and I have always had Provence on our bucket list, and with our good friends Pierre and Suzanne living part time in Avignon, we had the perfect excuse. Unfortunately, our time in this beautiful part of the world ends soon. We are heading back to Canada the day after tomorrow. Alain, how did you end up in this beautiful area?" Nathan queried, after lying about their departure date.

"Well it is somewhat of a long story, but the short version is that I was headhunted by a search firm on behalf of a local helicopter company, HELIVOL. I say local, but we sell choppers throughout the world. I was working with Bombardier at the time, as VP, logistics and transportation. As it turned out this was an area in which HELIVOL needed to improve, so I was offered the job as President here in Aix. I had recently divorced my wife, so I decided to take the plunge and move here," Alain described.

Nathan provided a brief synopsis of the governance work he did, where he was at, and where he had come from, and after Alain did the same, it was time to order off the menu. They ordered appetizers first. Nathan asked Alain if he would like wine with dinner and he indicated a red wine would be his preference. With the help of the sommelier, Nathan chose a finely aged bottle of Château de Pibaron, from the Bandol area in Provence. After a brief toast, they continued their conversation.

"Do you remember your hockey-playing days in Montreal? Did you play any hockey after high school?" Nathan asked.

"Not much really. I played for a while in a commercial league, and then some old-timers, but that was it. I hung up my skates when I came to Aix. How about you?"

Nathan related to Alain about his time playing hockey at university, and then his unusual but interesting experience playing for the *Jungle Jets* in Johannesburg. He followed-up telling the story of his friend Pierre's time as player/coach for the team in Villard-de-Lans, and Pierre's chance encounter with, and eventual marriage to Suzanne.

"You and I have something else in common – we both dated Kathy Borden – you in high school, and me in first year university. Do you remember that?" Nathan asked.

"Yes. What ever happened to her, do you know?"

"After we split-up she dated, and eventually married a friend of mine on the varsity football team. They moved to the USA and I lost track of them."

Nathan was swallowing hard throughout this encounter. While Alain had mellowed somewhat, Nathan still found him somewhat obnoxious. It might just be bad chemistry, or negative memories, Nathan thought. After a while, and more stories, they were served their main courses, paired with a second bottle of Château de Pibaron which they had half finished. Nathan was feeling the booze, and he could tell that Pelletier was as well. He noticed a slight change in Alain's demeanour as he became more aggressive. Nathan was not surprised with this, given his DNA.

"How do you enjoy living in France, Alain?" Nathan asked.

"Well, it is very different here. Things are done more flexibly. In Canada people are generally very Protestant, playing by the rules, whereas here people are more prepared to bend the rules. Even small things like getting a speeding ticket dropped by paying a few francs to a traffic cop is a readily tolerated practice," Pelletier responded.

"I see what you mean. In Canada we are more neurotic when it comes to things like that. Having done a number of consulting projects in different parts of the world – Kenya, Azerbaijan, and Russia come to mind – I have seen first hand as well how the world turns outside of Canada."

"Sounds like you have had an interesting career – your governance work paid for by hard-working taxpayers?"

"Mostly all of my work provides value-for-money for taxpayers because it increases the transparency and accountability of governments. I do work also for private sector clients, and my public sector assignments are often funded by organizations like the World Bank, the United Nations Office on Drugs & Crime, the International Monetary Fund, and the Financial Action Task Force," Nathan rebutted carefully.

"Yes, but multi-lateral institutions like those you mention are all funded by taxpayers, are they not?"

"True enough, indirectly they are through the taxes they pay to their individual member countries. If you don't mind me switching gears for a moment, I understand from my friend Pierre in Avignon that your company, HELIVOL, has an initiative that you are pushing to start helicopter test flights over Northern Provence," Nathan stated.

"Yes, that's right. It is becoming increasingly difficult to take our test flights south, over areas like Marseille, Toulon, and St. Tropez which, with recent population growth, are becoming large urban areas. With the missile silos being de-commissioned in Northern Provence, we think this is an ideal opportunity to move our test flights there, especially given the lower population density in the north. But we have had some pushback," Pelletier noted.

"Oh, pushback from whom?" Nathan asked with feigned innocence.

"A bunch of nutcases who don't care about jobs and the economy as long as they have the peaceful enjoyment of their property. Some of them are on the government dole and don't give a damn about working people. There is a semblance of a protest movement but we got rid of their leader thinking that would do the trick; but the group is still alive and kicking."

"When you say you got rid of their leader, is that the same person I read about in the local newspaper who was involved in a car accident in the Sault area?" again Nathan enquired with fake ignorance.

"Yes, that's the one – a Serge Dubois I believe – but I would hardly call it an accident. A few days after the incident, one of my guys traveled up to Sault and met with the Chief of the Sault Police Municipale. They sorted out a few things to make sure that anyone who may have thought the crash could have been deliberate would be placated. That is what I meant when I said that in this country things get sorted out with relative ease. It sometimes costs you, but that's business," Pelletier commented.

As Nathan was listening to Pelletier, he was thinking that what he had heard was as good as it could get. How incriminating it would be he didn't know, Nathan not being a lawyer, but he was sure that Louis would have some views on this.

"Interesting. Well, good luck with all of that. Switching gears for a moment again, if you don't mind, what do you do in your spare time in this neck of the woods?" queried Nathan.

"I don't really have much spare time per se, but when I do, I do some hiking and feed my photography habit. I am a keen photographer and this area is perfect for that. Apart from that, a bit of reading – mostly business journals and the international press."

The two of them continued with more small talk until around 11:30 p.m. when they decided to call it a day. They parted cordially, promising to stay in touch. Nathan went up to his hotel room, turned off the wire, and slept very well that night.

Chapter 39

Re-group

The next morning Nathan slept in and then read Le Figaro in bed. At 9 a.m. he wandered to the beautifully appointed outdoor pool at *La Villa Gallici*. He ordered breakfast and enjoyed it at a table beside the pool. How decadent! He was feeling very upbeat about what he felt was *mission accomplished*. In his hotel room later, he called Louis and arranged a time to go around to his home and hand off the listening device.

Nathan checked out, and after gasping when he saw the bill, headed to Louis' home.

"Bonjours, Louis. Ça vas bien?"

"Mais oui, et toi?"

"Great thanks. I think the dinner last night went well, but I will let you be the judge when you listen to the tape," Nathan said.

Louis took the wire from Nathan and placed the tape in his player. After listening to the tape, and based on cues from Nathan, fast forwarding to the key sections towards the end of the conversation, Louis commented,

"This is good. It is not absolutely categorical, but then again that was never our expectation. It is very damming. Like so many criminals, he just couldn't stop himself from bragging. It was astute of you to tell him that you were leaving the area very soon. He probably believed that preparing to leave, and then back in Canada, you would have other priorities and what he said would disappear quickly from your mind. I believe that what I need to do next is to meet with the Police Nationale here in Aix; show them what we have, and see if we can get them to request search warrants on the bank accounts of Maurice Bourke, real warrants this time, as well as the bank accounts of Alain Pelletier, HELIVOL corporate, and maybe HELIVOL's Vice-President Public Affairs, or equivalent, if they have one; and also the accounts of the Chief of Police in Sault, Captain Édouard Mercier. My guess is that HELIVOL paid a bribe to Mercier to cover-up the incriminating evidence. I believe that those people and HELIVOL make up the money trail. All payments would be made in cash, but the amounts are large ones and the search should be from early April until the end of June this year. I think a surprise visit by the Police Nationale to the Sault Police Municipale detachment, with a warrant in their back pocket to examine the physical evidence on site, and any correspondence or meetings with Pelletier, would be useful as well. I won't do anything yet, however, until we have our conference call, presumably in the next day or so," Louis said.

"That sounds good. I am heading back to Avignon after this. I will speak with Pierre and contact Jacques, and suggest a Skype conference call for tomorrow morning, and I will get in touch with you with the details."

"Parfait. In the meantime, I am going to create a transcription, verbatim, of the tape covering your dinner conversation with Pelletier so we have a hard copy for ourselves and for the Police Nationale. I will have this done by later today. Should I e-mail the document as an attachment to you, Pierre, and Jacques? I have a way to do this that will be secure, certainly from my end," Louis asked.

"Good idea. I think that it will be useful to have that in front of all of us when we speak tomorrow. I will ask the others to confirm that they are comfortable receiving the document electronically and I will advise you via e-mail early this afternoon."

That ended the meeting and Nathan headed back to Avignon in his rental car, arriving at the home of Pierre and Suzanne around noon. He related to Pierre the positive feeling he had about the dinner with Pelletier and suggested to him that they have a conference call the next morning. Pierre agreed and had no problem with the transcript being e-mailed to him. A telephone conversation with Jacques shortly afterwards confirmed all the arrangements for a Skype call, and the transcript transmission prior, for the next day at 10 a.m. Louis was also advised.

"So, it sounds like a successful, albeit expensive, foray into enemy territory," Pierre said with a smile on his face.

Nathan laughed, "Yes, I think so. We will have a good conversation tomorrow morning and nail down the next steps."

Suzanne interjected, "In the interim, how about some lunch? I have a cobb salad prepared. E'est-ce à votre goût?"

"I love cobbs. I am happy to join you for lunch here but on one condition – I would like to host the two of you for dinner tonight at a restaurant of your choosing," Nathan asserted.

"That is not necessary, but if you insist," Pierre chimed in.

"I do insist – please!"

"That is very kind. Pierre and I will choose a favourite restaurant and we promise that it will not be a Relais & Châteaux!" Suzanne promised.

It was another day of fantastic weather – too good to pass up eating outside on the back patio. When they were seated, relaxed, with their lunches in front of them, Suzanne kicked off the conversation.

"As you both know I am a bit of a political junkie, having studied political science at university, and yesterday I finished reading a very interesting book, *The Rise of China, How Economic Reform is Creating a New Superpower,* by William Overholt. Overholt is based in Hong Kong, where he serves as Managing Director of Bankers Trust Company. He has traveled widely in China and he holds a Ph.D. from Yale University. In this book he contrasts the *big bang* approach that was adopted with the fall of communism in the Soviet Union and Eastern Europe as they transformed their economies and political institutions; compared with the step-by-step transformation that was carefully and prudently launched by China. The end result is that Russia has floundered and China has taken off. Some have argued that the Soviets listened to the advice of westerners, including organizations like the World Bank and the IMF, and decided to simultaneously restructure their economy, the rule of law framework, and to a more limited extent their political institutions. China, on the other hand, moved more pragmatically, and for more or less obvious reasons left their political institutions intact and began a transformation of sorts of their economy in smaller bites. It is an interesting read and well researched."

Suzanne paused to allow the others to chime in. Nathan continued the discussion.

"The economic power that China has unleashed is staggering – soon to rival that of the USA," Nathan opined. "I believe that the Peoples Republic has very clear and ambitious geo-political goals. Many of the leadership of the Communist Party in China envisage China leading – not by revolution, but by global influence and actions, the reformation of the global governance system away from liberal democracy to authoritarian rule. By way of example, look at China's *One Belt, One Road* strategy, China's strategic global infrastructure program, which fundamentally challenges established norms around development financing and investment. The Chinese began these programs in Africa but they are now being extended into countries like Italy and Iran. These initiatives build loyalty and an opportunity for China to preach its ideology while *inside the tent* so to speak. On the economic front, for China to get to a point where the Yuan replaces the US dollar as the global currency that is accepted for trade throughout the world would, I believe, be a highly desired outcome for them. This would be a stretch goal and would require China to reach a point when, if ever, its economy significantly surpasses that of the USA," Nathan concluded.

"Interesting, and perhaps scary, thoughts," Pierre commented. "I'm not paranoid about the Peoples Republic of China, but on the question of militarism, one reads a lot these days about the huge build-up of the Chinese navy in the Pacific. I wonder, will they ever surpass the US military might in the area, and if they do, what are the implications? Would they be able to fulfill any ambitions they have in that area with respect to Taiwan, or to accessing oil and gas assets in the South China Sea?"

"It seems to me," Suzanne followed, "based on what I have read, that China is still a very long way off to surpass the naval strength of the US, and by inference the so-called *West*, in the Pacific. Size of the fleet is one thing, but the USA is technologically much more advanced. I would not suggest for a minute, however, that China is not capable of catching up, but it will take a while. Not to add more fuel to the fire, but in the news we have been hearing about negotiations taking place as we speak between China and the World Trade Organization which could lead to China's accession to the WTO. I believe the discussions began in 1995. If China does join this international trading system, I wonder how successful it will be in moving to a market economy. This will mean removing tariff and non-tariff trade barriers, opening its markets to foreign companies, eliminating subsidies, respecting intellectual property rights and the rule of law, and addressing concerns alleged by the Americans – probably true – about currency manipulation to favour its trade balance. These would be huge challenges, and, quite frankly I am not convinced that China can implement the changes that they will be required to commit to. They will also have to take actions to significantly reduce or eliminate the plethora of counterfeit goods leaving China and ending up around the world – some creating serious health and safety problems."

The three of them sat around and tried to solve the world's problems as they enjoyed the cobb salad. After a short nap that afternoon, followed by a sundowner on the patio, they headed off to a charming restaurant – *La Cuisine du Dimanche* – where they enjoyed a great meal. Nathan had a Cassoulet, a dish that he had come to enjoy when he did project work in Strasbourg for the European Parliament. Suzanne had a salade Niçoise, and Pierre topped the selections off with a boeuf bourguignon. A good time was had by all.

Chapter 40

On we go

Pierre and Nathan huddled over the speaker phone in Pierre's study as they connected to the other two on the Skype conference call.

"Bonjours tout le monde," Jacques welcomed them from his home in Paris.

They all reciprocated the salutations and after some small talk, Jacques opened up the dialogue about the affairs at hand.

"First, I think we should we discuss the transcript that Louis sent us giving a verbatim record of Nathan's dinner talk with Pelletier. Then we should turn to Louis to discuss where we go from here. With respect to the transcript, I thought Nathan had some great success in getting information out of Pelletier. It exceeded my expectations but Nathan set the whole thing up well, and Pelletier's lips loosened up nicely as the drinks went down. I am looking forward to Pierre, Nathan, and Louis' assessment, and Louis' advice on where we go next."

Pierre jumped in, "Nathan told me that Pelletier downed a double scotch and a bottle of wine at the dinner table so that would probably explain the loss of inhibition. Well done, Nathan. I am with you, Jacques. The more Pelletier talked, the more elated I became. I think we have some great incriminating evidence here, but Louis will be the better judge of that."

"I was really pleased with the way the evening went," Nathan offered. "Pelletier's offensive nature emerged as more Château de Pibaron passed his lips. Many people show those same characteristics – they become more aggressive when they drink. In any case, Pelletier cooperated well, I think."

"OK, we seem to be in agreement that we have something quite constructive to work with. What are your thoughts, Louis, and how do we use this information, and all of the other material that you have collected, to good advantage?" Jacques asked.

"Nathan did some fine work at *La Villa Gallici.* We have some very good material to work with there, together with that from Bourke, and the information that Jacques got from junior Constable, Claude Laurin, from the Sault Police Municipale detachment, a while ago. What I suggest is that, with your permission, I will arrange a meeting with a friend, and former colleague of mine, Gabriel Brodeur, who works with the Police Nationale here in Aix. He is an inspecteur, or detective in English, and he is very competent. His integrity is beyond reproach. This last quality will be important because I think the Police Municipale in Sault will need to be challenged. Although there is some rivalry between these two forces, it is never easy to take on a fellow police officer. In advance of my meeting with Brodeur, I will develop a briefing note for them describing what we have to date. I will share this with all of you as well. My *asks* will be for them to seek search warrants on the bank accounts of Maurice Bourke, as well as the bank accounts of Alain Pelletier, HELIVOL corporate bank accounts, and HELIVOL's Vice-President Public Affairs; and, also the accounts of the Chief of Police in Sault, Captain Édouard Mercier. My guess is that HELIVOL paid a bribe to Mercier to cover-up the incriminating evidence. As I said to Nathan yesterday, I believe that those people and HELIVOL make up the money trail. The searches should be from early April until the end of June this year. I think a surprise visit by the Police Nationale to the Sault Police Municipale detachment, with a warrant in their back pocket to examine the physical evidence on site, and a trail of any correspondence or meetings with Pelletier, would be useful as well. So, that is what I am proposing. Are we in agreement, or do you have any questions or concerns?" Louis concluded.

"This all sounds solid," Jacques said. "Two questions from me; Firstly, do you envisage lie detector tests coming into play; and, secondly, assuming for the moment that the money trail is confirmed, and Bourke's fender is located in the Sault Police Municipale detachment evidence room, in your judgement is there enough to secure convictions, and if yes, against whom and for what?"

Louis stepped in, "It's too early to say whether or not a lie detector will need to be employed. That will depend on the police. It can be a useful tool, in particular to try and resolve contradictory claims by suspects or witnesses. On your second point, at a minimum, depending again on how the police and prosecutors view this, there is a 'leaving the scene of the accident' charge against Bourke assuming the fender assembly is located and connected with his car and/or he does not recant his previous story. Then, it seems to me manslaughter, and conspiracy to commit manslaughter – if conspiracy can be tied to a charge of manslaughter – at a minimum seem likely for Bourke and Pelletier respectively. These two charges can be elevated to murder if all the stars align. Much of this is tied to whether or not there was intent to commit murder or, alternatively, serious bodily harm – this is the stuff of lawyers. We will know better on this point within the next week or so. There is also potentially a charge of obstruction of justice and betrayal of the public trust against the Chief of Police in Sault, Captain Édouard Mercier. That is how I see things stacking up at this point, but there is still some work to be done and the ultimate charges laid could be at variance with this. It is often hard to predict."

"Thanks, that answers my questions. Any other questions or comments friends?" Jacques asked.

"None from here is Avignon. We look forward to the briefing document from Louis, and to the next conference call when he has something to report," Pierre commented.

"That being the case, we will end the call. Bonne chance, Louis. Please keep us posted. Au revoir," Jacques ended the call.

After drinking a cup of coffee, Louis began to work on his laptop to develop the brief he had referred to in the conference call. Once completed, he e-mailed the report to Jacques, Nathan and Pierre and he invited their comment. In the interim, he placed a call into Inspecteur Gabriel Brodeur, at the Police Nationale in Aix.

"Bonjours Gabriel. Ici Louis Prud'-homme."

"Mais oui, bonjours. Ça fait un moment nous n'avons pas parlé."

"Yes, it has been a while. I would like to come and see you at your office, if possible, sometime this week if you are available. As you know, I am working as a private investigator and I have some information that will be of interest to you," Louis said.

"For you Louis, pas de problème."

A date and time were set for two days hence for the meeting.

Chapter 41

The plumber

It was raining hard the day when Louis met with Inspecteur Gabriel Brodeur, at the offices of the Police Nationale in Aix. After a few pleasantries and a couple of stories from the past, Louis handed Brodeur a copy of the brief he had prepared and walked him through the document. The brief included the transcript of the dinner conversation between Nathan and Pelletier.

After listening to Louis' presentation and asking a couple of questions along the way, the Inspecteur said facetiously, "Well clearly, *Something is rotten in the state of Denmark* here, but it is not Denmark, it is in Provence, France!"

"I couldn't agree with you more," Louis concurred.

"I will need a few days to go over the material, digest it, review it with colleagues, and then make a recommendation to my boss. I anticipate that we should be able to convince a judge to issue the search warrants you have suggested, but I will not pre-judge that. Please, leave it with me for the time being, and I will be in touch when I have something to report," Brodeur said.

"Ça marche très bien pour moi. Merci beaucoup, Gabriel. You know how to reach me so I will await your call. If you have any questions, or need some clarification, do not hesitate to call me," Louis concluded.

Reaching his home, Louis sent an e-mail to the group telling them that the file was in the hands of the police. He told them that his contact had reacted positively to the brief, in the sense that he agreed that there was definitely something suspicious going on which required investigating. They had to wait for the police to review the matter in more detail. The police would call Louis when that was complete.

Back in Avignon, Nathan had made contact with Fairmont's Vice-President of Business Development, Cameron Sutton, to get an update on their review process, and if they needed the assistance of Pierre and/or himself. Cameron told Nathan that they had zeroed in on three locations in Northern Provence – one just outside Sault, another on the outskirts of Apt, and the third just north of Simiane la Rotunde. They had taken out options on three parcels of land and had met with two architects that they had shortlisted. They had chosen one and were working with that firm on design concepts and architectural drawings. The architect had introduced the Fairmont team to a quantity surveyor and an engineer who had provided them with enough information to develop capital cost estimates. They were quite enthusiastic about the project, especially about the business prospects in the northern part of

Provence – away from the saturated south. They wished now to meet with the local Chambres de Commerce, and also with officials in Marseille, the capital of the administrative region of Provence-Alpes-Cote d'Azur. Meetings with local government officials in Sault, Apt, and Simiane la Rotunde were also on their radar. They were anxious to meet also with the HELIVOL protest group that Serge had led before his untimely death.

Pierre had kept in contact with the protest group, and in particular with the new unofficial leader, Victor, who had stepped in following Serge's demise. Nathan suggested to Cameron that Pierre could make the introductions to Victor and the protest group, help set up a meeting, and attend it himself. Nathan proposed that, following that meeting, Pierre and Victor would help the Fairmont team organize the meetings with the Chambers of Commerce and the government officials. Given their knowledge of the local area, and their fluency in French, Nathan felt they could both be put to good use. He was not sure what he himself could add at this time. Cameron was very happy with that approach. Nathan undertook to confirm this arrangement with Pierre and Victor and call Cameron back that afternoon or early the next day.

Nathan discussed the proposition with Pierre and secured his agreement. This was followed by a call from Pierre to Victor who was very keen to meet the Fairmont group and be of whatever assistance he could. Nathan re-confirmed all of this with Cameron.

In conversation with Pierre, Nathan expressed the view that he was now somewhat redundant in Provence until they heard back from the police. He planned to return to Toronto, unless Pierre had other ideas.

"You are more than welcome to stay here in Avignon, but I hear what you are saying," Pierre commented.

"That is very kind, but I will head back to Canada tomorrow. I have a few things I need to deal with there, and it will be great to see Erika again."

The next day, Nathan said his goodbyes and hopped on the TGV to Paris and on an Air Canada flight from Charles de Gaulle to Toronto.

At home on the Kingsway, he and Erika caught up on all of the news over dinner. It was great to be home thought Nathan. Erika reminded him that they had a renovation contractor tentatively booked to come to their home in a few days time to update their three bathrooms. Their home in the Kingsway in Toronto was stately and old, but the water closets were in need of some work – probably the original versions were still in place.

"I have an idea that I would like to discuss with the plumber," Nathan proposed.

"What is that, darling," Erika replied.

"Well, you know Byron Finlayson, a fellow Rotarian, owns a plumbing supplies shop and I bet he could give us a very good deal on toilets and sinks."

"Would that be acceptable to the plumber who is coming to replace those items? He might wish to source his own materials," Erika asked.

Nathan agreed that could be an issue and called the plumber the next day. The plumber was very familiar with the Finlayson shop and told Nathan that he had no problem buying the toilets and sinks there, at prices negotiated by Nathan. He would simply flow-through these items at his cost, and charge for his labour at his normal rates. "Not a problem," he said. He supplied Nathan with the part numbers that Finlayson's would use.

Nathan had been a member of the local Rotary International Club for many years. In fact, during his tenure there he and Erika had hosted five different exchange students – two from Finland, one from Germany, one from Colombia and one from Mexico. They typically stayed for three or four months at each home and were rotated amongst the local membership for a full academic school year. It was a great experience for the students, and for the hosts as well. Byron had participated in the program as well, and the two of them got along well.

The next day Nathan reached Byron at his warehouse office. After a short cordial discussion Nathan put his proposition to Byron. He supplied Byron with the part numbers and was given the wholesale price quotation – the lower price he would charge plumbers.

"I will do this for you, but I am not supposed to. The wholesale price is for plumbers only, and they would not be happy if they knew I was doing this."

"Many thanks, Byron. Much appreciated."

Nathan then called the plumber back and told him he could pick up the items any time. A few days later the plumber showed up at their house and began the work, after another contractor had completed the flooring, lighting, and built new showers.

Nathan's plumber was back and forth to their home over the next many days and Nathan was not very pleased with his stop-and-go modus operandi. He spoke to the plumber about it and was told that glues needed to dry, etc. Nathan suspected that he was juggling a number of jobs and that was what explained his disappearances. Nathan asked him to speed up the process and decided to leave it at that.

Nathan was surprised at the prices he was being charged for the sinks and toilets when the plumber's first invoice arrived. He called Byron to check out the prices.

"Oh, no, those prices are about thirty per cent higher than what we charged your plumber," Byron asserted.

"But how can that be? My plumber has attached your invoice to his bill and that is the price he has charged me," Nathan questioned in a puzzled tone.

"Something else I should not tell you is that it sometimes happens that we charge a plumber for supplies with an inflated price; and then we turn around and issue a credit note to him. So, the plumber charges his or her customer the inflated price, purportedly at his or her cost, and then pays us the lower price. A bit of a shell game that is quite common in the trade, I am embarrassed to say. Not aligned at all with Rotary's values I am afraid. Again, you mustn't repeat this, and please do not act on this," Byron pleaded.

"My lips are sealed but thank you."

Nathan was furious. He called the plumber on his cell phone.

"You are fired. I want you off the job. Please come and collect any tools you have left here. I have not appreciated your work habits and I am not pleased with the prices you have charged me for the sinks and toilets," Nathan said confidently.

The plumber was irate.

"But sir, I charged you for materials at my cost from Finlayson's. The invoice is attached to my bill."

"I am not getting into the details but I am not happy with your services and they are terminated," Nathan said authoritatively.

Later that day Byron called Nathan back and asked him to repeat the part numbers.

"Nathan, I am so sorry but when you called, I was up to my neck in alligators, and I gave you the wrong numbers. The prices charged by your plumber are the right ones – the prices we charged him. I hope you haven't used the information I gave you earlier to take any action," Byron questioned.

Nathan had to be careful because he had promised to keep the information confidential and not to act on it. There are times when one must tell a little white lie.

"No, of course not."

"Whew, thank goodness, and again my apologies," Byron said.

Nathan felt uncomfortable about what he had said to the plumber. It was acceptable for Nathan to be unhappy with the plumber's work habits, but obviously he had been completely honest about the prices on the supplies. Nathan had severe pangs of guilt which led him to pick up the phone.

"Hi. Listen, I have an apology to make. What I said about the pricing of the supplies was totally inaccurate and inappropriate. I don't know how I jumped to that conclusion. I won't renege, however, on my unhappiness about how long the job was taking, so our deal is finished. I just wanted you to know, however, what the real reason was," Nathan said uncomfortably.

"I really appreciate the call because I was completely flummoxed over your unhappiness with my pricing of the materials. Have a great day."

Nathan recalled what the German writer and statesman Johann Wolfgang von Goethe once said – *By seeking and blundering we learn.*

Chapter 42

Wrapping things up

Ten days after he had met with Inspecteur Gabriel Brodeur Louis had a call back. L'Inspecteur reported that within the Police Nationale Department in Aix, they were agreed with the need for the search warrants that Louis had recommended, and that an application to that effect had been made to a local judge, who had approved them. The warrant covering the Sault Police Municipale would only be used if needed. Local police detachments would typically cooperate with the Police Nationale, the federal force, so the warrant would be used there only as a last resort. Inspecteur Brodeur also reported that police officers had already been deployed to the banks in question, and two officers had traveled to Sault to conduct a surprise visit of the municipale detachment. As soon as they had some results to report on, the inspecteur undertook to contact Louis. Louis thanked him profusely and conveyed this information to Nathan, Pierre and Jacques.

Pierre and Victor had been doing some traveling with the Fairmont team and the reception they had been receiving from the Chambres du Commerce and government officials was very positive. Most saw the Fairmont proposal, when compared to the HELIVOL alternative, as more labour intensive, primarily with high quality jobs, and it came with a smaller environmental footprint than helicopter test flights. They also saw the multiplier effect associated with the health spas as much more pronounced when one took into consideration the local supply chain demands that the spas would exert covering items like food & wine, supplies, cleaning, transportation, and the like. They did acknowledge, however, that HELIVOL was already a major player in the area and one to be reckoned with.

As they went along, the Fairmont team was drafting the key parts of the bankable investment grade feasibility study that they were committed to developing. Good information had been forthcoming from the local architects, engineers, and quantity surveyors. The group back in Toronto was fine-tuning the sales and marketing piece, and the human resources costed plan. Fairmont had also enjoyed a very productive and lively session with the HELIVOL NON protest group that Victor had organized at the outset. Their passion and commitment were obvious and some of the research they had conducted, and information they had assembled, came in handy as they were doing the rounds and meeting with government officials.

Pierre had largely concluded his work with the Fairmont team so it was agreed that he could head back home to Avignon. Victor would be available to the team if required. Pierre was anxious to get back to Avignon and finish his garden shed and gazebo before he and Suzanne headed back to Montréal.

Pierre and Suzanne would miss the Jazz Festival in Montreal that year, but there was so much to do in the city that they loved. They often strolled in Mount Royal Park where, on a clear day, Montreal was visible for miles. They enjoyed the cosmopolitan flavour of Montreal, with its mix of Anglophones, Francophones, and Allophones from many countries around the world. Le Musée des beaux-arts de Montréal was very close to where Pierre and Suzanne lived on Sherbrooke Street. They frequently stopped in there, especially to see special exhibits that were shown often. Pierre was an adoring fan of Les Canadiens de Montréal hockey club (the *Habs* short for Les Habitants) and he was just getting used to the Bell Centre as the *Habs* home ice that replaced the Montreal Forum – often referred to as the Mecca of ice hockey. Pierre and Suzanne enjoyed eating out at the great restaurants in Vieux-Montréal. In short, a wonderful place to call home.

In Aix, Louis was called to a meeting at the offices of the Police Nationale. At the meeting with Inspecteur Gabriel Brodeur and others, he was given a complete update on the status of their investigation into the Serge Dubois matter. Following the meeting, he called Pierre in Avignon and suggested a Skype conference call for the next day. The timing would work for Pierre since he and Suzanne would still be in Avignon. Pierre communicated with Jacques and Nathan and the call was set up for 2 pm the next day.

Chapter 43

Unravel

Jacques welcomed Pierre, Nathan, and Louis to the call the next day, and after a few pleasantries, Jacques turned the floor over to Louis.

"Louis, I understand that you have some news. Alors, vous avez la parole," Jacques opened.

"Merci Jacques. Yes, I had a very productive meeting yesterday with Inspecteur Gabriel Brodeur and his colleagues at the Police Nationale offices in Aix. There are several things to cover. As I communicated to you previously, the police acted on the search warrants and they completed a surprise visit to the Sault Police Municipale detachment. By going through the bank records, they confirmed the amounts that were deposited into Bourke's bank account. An initial 50,000 francs was discovered at the end of April. Bourke had told Louis that he kept 15,000 of the 65,000 francs in his pocket. The remaining balance of 65,000 francs was deposited on May 22, two days after Serge died. Once they had these specific dates nailed down it narrowed the time frame that they needed to search the bank records of HELIVOL, Alain Pelletier, and HELIVOL's VP Public Affairs."

"What did they find?" Nathan asked.

Louis continued, "With those parameters they located the corresponding cash withdrawals from the bank account of Alain Pelletier, not HELIVOL's bank, just days before these two deposits into Bourke's account. It is interesting that Pelletier took this on himself and shows how important it was to him personally. Going through HELIVOL also had its risks and potential to backfire, so he may have thought it wisest to pay the fee himself. Obviously, he doesn't suffer financially. Inspecteur Brodeur followed up by interviewing Bourke and Pelletier but I will come back to that in a moment. The officers also found an amount of 50,000 francs being withdrawn from Pelletier's bank account on May 23rd, and a deposit for 48,000 francs deposited into Édouard Mercier's bank account on the 25th of May."

"Carry on," Jacques commented.

"Simultaneously with the work that I just described, two police officers traveled to Sault and, without warning, asked to speak with the Chief of Police in Sault, Captain Édouard Mercier. Apparently, he was quite surprised and taken aback. Initially he refused access to the two Police Nationale officers based on some flimsy and inappropriate excuse about inadequate notice, but when the officers pulled out the search warrant, he naturally complied. When the evidence box from the May 19 crash was reviewed by the two officers, they quickly came upon the fender and headlight assembly, together with the additional photographs taken at the scene of the accident. The *new* photos portrayed the extensive scratches and dents on the left side of Serge's car. These previously undeclared pieces of evidence were taken back to Aix and examined by forensic scientists. Their work confirmed that the fender assembly did indeed match the body parts replaced by the body shop *Auto Plus* on Bourke's car. The scratches and dents added weight to the conclusion that Bourke's car had deliberately run Serge's car off the road."

"As we had anticipated," Nathan intervened.

"Yes. Now to the police interviews with Bourke, Pelletier and Mercier. Bourke basically repeated what he had told me previously. He also stuck to his story that the plan had been to intimidate Serge, not to kill him. The discussion with Pelletier was apparently quite interesting. At first, he denied everything, but with the evidence of the bank deposits, Bourke's story, and excerpts from the transcript from his dinner with Nathan, he changed his tune. He was absolutely staggered and furious about the taped dinner conversation. He kept saying that it was an infringement of his rights, etc. saying, 'What a loser that Nathan Callahan was. I always knew it. Who was he working for, anyway?' But then he finally came around and admitted that Serge was a pain in the ass to him and he wanted to intimidate him so that he would *pull his dogs off.* When the officers challenged him on this point and said that he wanted Serge dead, he denied this. On the matter of the payment to Mercier, when officers confronted Pelletier about the withdrawal and deposit, he said that he got his man Charles Camus to pay a visit to the Sault Municipale Police detachment. He said he told Camus to pay Captain Mercier the 50,000 francs to help him out with his investigation. The officers thought, how magnanimous, but this story did not align with the confession from Mercier who, when confronted with the evidence, admitted to withholding evidence from the police report that he had originally sent to Jacques in return for the bribe. The Chief was despondent and very upset when he made these admissions, officers reported. Faced with this, Pelletier confessed to this crime also."

"Wow, what a tangled web," Pierre commented.

Louis continued, "I'll say! The Police Nationale officers were very busy and they did some exceptional work. Now I will need to tell you about the discussions the police have had to date with the prosecutors, or ministère publique."

Louis continued with his description of the status of the investigation.

"Gentlemen, this is what the police have told me. The prosecutors believe that a murder charge will not stick for Bourke or Pelletier because of their inability to prove intent. For a charge of murder to stick, one has to prove that the intent was to do so, to end a life. Both suspects have stuck to their story that their intention was simply to intimidate. Prosecutors also felt that Pelletier's comment over dinner with Nathan, 'but I would hardly call it an accident', was not enough to prove intent. Bourke will be charged with manslaughter which, in France, is punishable by fifteen to twenty years in prison. When it comes to sentencing, prosecutors will ask the judge to shave off a couple of years off Bourke's sentence because he cooperated with police by implicating the major culprit, Pelletier."

"Even if they are not charged with murder, they will both be behind bars for some time," Jacques interjected.

"Absolutely right, Jacques," Louis continued, "the situation with Pelletier, according to the lawyers, is a little but more complicated and they have not reached a conclusion yet. In a common law country, one might look to a charge of conspiracy, but the concept of conspiracy is different in France, where the civil code prevails. The lawyers are contemplating a charge of either accomplice, accessory, or aiding and abetting. An accomplice is criminally liable to the same extent as the principal, in this case fifteen to twenty years in prison, so this is where the prosecutors are leaning. To that one would add, for the bribe that Pelletier paid to the Chief of Police in Sault, Captain Édouard Mercier, a charge of bribery of a domestic public official which is punishable under French law by a 10-year term of imprisonment and a fine of 5 million French francs. So, any way one looks at it, Pelletier will be behind bars for some time."

Louis paused. "Any comments or concerns so far?"

Hearing none, he continued. "Captain Mercier will be convicted of taking a bribe and betraying a public trust, and he will lose his job and pension rights. At this time the French civil code is evolving, and one area in particular that is in a state of flux is the amount of time in jail for a public official who takes a bribe. The French government and l'Assemblée Nationale are beginning to take a much harder line on bribery and corruption. The current thinking is that he or she who took the bribe should have the same prison time as the person who paid the bribe. In this case that would be ten years. Even if a shorter sentence is meted out under the current law, a charge of obstruction of justice for misrepresenting a vehicle accident report will likely be added. Camus will also be facing charges for aiding and abetting," Louis asserted.

"The Junior Constable, Claude Laurin, who works at the Sault Police Municipale detachment, the one who telephoned Jacques and told him that some of the evidence was missing in the accident report that Édouard Mercier sent to him, will be protected under the French whistleblower legislation which precludes criminal prosecution for releasing the information he did, and against any possible repercussions by his employer."

"I am so glad to hear that," Jacques said, "because I gave my word to Laurin that I would treat the information he gave to me with absolute discretion. He did the right thing."

Louis continued, "Based on these charges, Bourke, Pelletier and Mercier were arrested yesterday. I believe Pelletier and Mercier are out on bail. Pelletier has relinquished his passport and he has had other restrictions placed on him. I think that wraps it up for me. Any questions or concerns?"

"Louis, I think you have done an incredible job. My brother, Serge, rest his soul, will see justice done. It won't bring him back but it will hold accountable those who caused his death. For that you will receive a bonus above and beyond your contract amount. I will discuss this with Nathan and Pierre later and add the bonus to your final bill," Jacques offered.

Nathan and Pierre jumped in and expressed total agreement. They wrapped up the call with a request from Louis to keep them apprised of any major developments if and when they occurred. Louis agreed to do this, and thanked Jacques and the others for the opportunity to work with them. He had enjoyed and benefited from the experience. He invited all of them to visit him in Aix when they were next in that part of the world. He told the group that he was looking forward to re-connecting with his old friend Arthur Petit, the *Auto Plus* owner in Aix.

After the call, Jacques communicated with Nathan and Pierre and told them he would pay Louis a bonus of 10,000 francs for his hard, and effective work. Pierre and Nathan thought this was totally appropriate and they both offered to top it up. Jacques declined this offer on the basis that Serge was his brother, and he had taken responsibility for the contract. Pierre and Nathan thanked Jacques and they promised to stay in touch and looked forward to a reunion one day in Paris, Toronto, Montreal, Simiane la Rotunde, or Aix – or wherever.

In Toronto, Nathan had organized a meeting the next day with Fairmont's Vice-President of Business Development, Cameron Sutton, at Fairmont's downtown office. The team was back from Provence and had some news for Nathan.

Nathan learned the next day that Cameron and the team had completed the bankable investment grade feasibility study and the numbers looked good, indicating a solid return on investment. In fact, the Fairmont Board of Directors had approved the project and construction would begin on the spa in the Sault area within the next few months. The other two locations would be locked in, and be phased in over the next two years. Business conditions for the company were improving so the expansion would be financed with internal financial cash flow and resources. Fairmont was very bullish on this project and it had broad support throughout the organization – and in the holding company as well.

Nathan reflected on how pleased Serge would be, looking down from above, to see these health spas being built in Northern Provence – his dream come true. His sacrifice had not been in vain. As Jacques had noted as well, the perpetrators of the crimes that caused his death were being brought to justice.

Throughout this initiative Nathan wondered to himself what had kept him interested and involved in this exercise. Apart from his desire to discover the truth behind Serge's death and to see that justice was done, he held a conviction that the health spa project made so much more sense for Northern Provence than helicopter test flights. Learning that his former nemesis, Allan, now Alain, Pelletier was behind the helicopter proposal, and ultimately behind Serge's death, was an added motivation to stay engaged. Nathan had never seen himself as a vindictive person, and certainly the rough relationship that Allan and Nathan had in high school would never justify, in Nathan's mind, the end to Pelletier's life that was unfolding – with many years behind bars. The truth was, however, that notwithstanding any childhood grudge that Nathan may have had against Allan, this man had orchestrated the murder of someone, Serge, who was simply expressing his freedom of choice and speech. Pelletier had also bribed a public official which Nathan found abhorrent as well. Nathan was glad that he had stayed with this project to completion, even though it had cost him time and money.

Were there any negatives to all that had transpired over the last few weeks? Nathan pondered. Well, Jacques was faced with Louis' bill for services rendered; Pierre would have to work overtime to complete the construction of his gazebo and garden shed; and Nathan would have to find another plumber!

Acknowledgements

Thanks to my wife, Ethne, for her encouragement and support in writing this book, and for her review and critique.

Over the years I have met, and been associated with, many exceptional people. I have also had opportunities to involve myself in a variety of interesting and challenging issues, and life experiences. In this book I have woven some of these stories into the main plot line. I hope the reader will excuse me for these indulgences, and that you have enjoyed these sidebars as much as I have delighted in telling them.

Thank you also to Mitchel Anderson and Joseph Ragaza at Tellwell Publishing.

CPSIA information can be obtained
at www.ICGtesting.com
Printed in the USA
BVHW081344030820
585345BV00003B/19

9 780228 837275